"*BFFs* is a story we can all see ourselves in and learn from. I laughed out loud and even teared up in a few parts (don't tell anyone). Jennifer's book takes the reader on an unexpected journey to discover the value of each person, to see an individual's unlimited potential, and to focus on what really matters in life. Knowing Jennifer personally, I see her real life character, passion, and energy come through in these pages. For a meaningful read with fun, drama, and surprises, *BFFs* is a can't miss."

James Baker
*Pastor, Real Estate Investor, Family Man*

"In her novella, *BFFs: Best Friends Forever*, Jennifer Calvert, Lower School Guidance Counselor at Cannon School in Concord, N.C., not only addresses the problem of bullying in schools, but provides strategies for dealing with a bully. Any middle school student or parent of a middle school student who has lived the role of a victim of bullying should read this book. Jennifer's passion for helping students who are victims of bullying is evident as the story unfolds. It is a quick read and one that you do not want to miss."

Gay Roberts
*35 years experience in education.*
*She currently serves as Lower School Head at*
*Cannon School in Concord, North Carolina.*

# BFFs
## BEST FRIENDS FOREVER

To the Jenkes Family,

I've enjoyed knowing you guys. You are all such a sweet, kind family. Las Stockton God has great plans for your life!.

Much love,
Mrs. Calvert

TATE PUBLISHING
*& Enterprises*

Tate Publishing is committed to excellence in the publishing industry. Our staff of highly trained professionals, including editors, graphic designers, and marketing personnel, work together to produce the very finest books available. The company reflects the philosophy established by the founders, based on Psalms 68:11,

"THE LORD GAVE THE WORD AND GREAT WAS THE COMPANY OF THOSE WHO PUBLISHED IT."

If you would like further information, please contact us:

1.888.361.9473 | www.tatepublishing.com

TATE PUBLISHING *& Enterprises*, LLC | 127 E. Trade Center Terrace Mustang, Oklahoma 73064 USA

ISBN: 978-1-6024715-1-1
07.02.08

# BFFs
### BEST FRIENDS FOREVER

JENNIFER E. CALVERT

TATE PUBLISHING & *Enterprises*

To my husband, Dave, who is the most unselfish person I've ever known. I love you!

To my daughter, Cassie, may your heart always pursue things that matter for eternity; you are a blessing! I love you!

To my friend, Sherylle, who was like a midwife on this book, helping birth it and bring it to life. What a friend! Thanks for all the gazillion hours you spent helping me.

To my dad, Dr.; Col. Wallace Early, who has all "the right stuff," and truly is a hero by example and deed. Thank you for all your many blessings! I love you!

# ACKNOWLEDGEMENTS

I would like to thank the following people who took time to read my manuscript and make suggestions: Beverly Hartman, Tracy Wade, Elizabeth Northrup, LeAnna Kim Smith, Cassie and Dave Calvert, Jan and Amy Hurndon, Courtney Broocks, Deby Jizi, Deborah Starczewski, Larry Heath, Gay Roberts, Jim Baker, and Mary Collins.

A huge thanks to Jackie Taylor and Sherylle Smith for helping me edit the manuscript and encouraging me to persevere with Jennifer's story and see it published.

Also, a gigantic thanks to the "real" Jennifer for allowing me to tell her story in order to help others avoid the pain she suffered. Finally, to my students at Cannon School who found Jennifer's story powerful and wanted to see it made into a book.

# TABLE OF CONTENTS

# FOREWORD

Frequently when I tell people for the first time that I am a middle school teacher, they cringe and usually ask, "Why? Are you crazy?" I am not insulted; I completely understand why they react this way. I have taught middle school for twenty-plus years—I probably am crazy! But even during the most insane moments at middle school, I know, somewhere in my soul, that the student himself faces far more challenges than I.

These are the years that adolescents face a plethora of issues: intellectual and physical changes, peer pressure, and self-identity. Middle school students themselves, however, focus more on social status and fitting in, just being accepted. Unfortunately, the menace of bullying, which usually begins in lower school, becomes more prevalent and more vicious in later years, and choices are more difficult to make.

All of us have known at least one bully or perhaps have been one. We know that bullies carefully choose their victims; they harass and ridicule them both publicly and privately, and they are relentless.

If the target is lucky, a courageous student comes forward and offers support, if not defense. That student immediately puts himself at risk of becoming a target or a pariah.

Sadly, we also are acquainted with the tragedies associated with teenage drinking and driving. Each of us, I'm sure, can tell at least one incident of a friend, classmate, or relative involved in an alcohol-related accident that left a teenager maimed or crippled or worse. We teachers all too often weep for young lives lost or changed forever because students made the wrong choice simply because they wanted to be popular or they feared ostracism.

Speaking up is difficult, whether it is against bullying or underage drinking. In *BFFs: Best Friends Forever*, Mrs. Calvert, herself a parent of a middle school student and school counselor, follows a group of students from middle school through high school and in the process teaches lessons in courage, acceptance, and faith. I recommend *BFFs* to students and parents and suggest that they read it as a family. It is a book that can be used as a tool to open discussions about bullying, teenage drinking, and making choices.

Jackie Taylor
*Master Teacher, 28 years experience*
*teaching middle and high school*

# INTRODUCTION

Have you ever been inside a middle school and experienced all of the fun, anxiety, stress, and pressure that the typical middle school student and teacher experiences? If not, this is your chance to be involved in the lives of a number of students, teachers, parents, and community agencies that are linked to this most critical developmental age in children.

This story is about real people who experience life-changing miracles. Jennifer Calvert has creatively written a story about a serious problem in our public and private schools: bullying in middle school. She has confidently found answers to this issue. This story is about relationships and how they impact parent-child, teacher-student, student-student, teacher-parent, church and community. The values that form character in our students are addressed in an open and honest story set in a local community in a local middle school with all the relationships that can be found there. This book needs to be read by parents, students, and teachers. The importance of roles, relationships and the values that students, need to into mature caring, responsible persons are resourcefully and ingeniously revealed in this fascinating story. The value of seeing an individual as special, created by God, with purpose in life is an important responsibility of parents, students, teachers, and the community. It also involves the community of faith.

Larry M. Heath

Larry Heath has served in the local church ministry for over 40 years. Having served eight churches in two major denominations, he has extensive experience in pastoral counseling, marriage and family enrichment, and support group ministries. Much of his ministry is devoted to individual, couple, and family counseling; marriage enrichment seminars and retreats; and small group leadership training. His writings and small group materials on anger have been used in churches, court systems, community groups, and schools both in America and other countries.

He is the author of two books on anger management:

*Anger: Our Master or Our Servant–The Creative Use of a Powerful Emotion*

*Mastering Anger: A Guide for Family and Friends.*

Abby bounded up the stairs to her office, her running clothes drenched in sweat from her ten-mile run, the Secret Service agents puffing hard behind her. Her running kept her looking at least ten years younger than her true age of forty-eight. Wrinkles had yet to inhabit her face. Her long, blonde hair swept back in a ponytail remained luminescent.

"Any messages, Cassie?" Abby asked her personal secretary who had been with Abby since she was a senator. Cassie was like a daughter to Abby and her husband, Brett.

"Yes, Madame President, you had two messages."

"What were they?"

"Well, the first was from a Ryan Rydell, who asked if you could use your influence to persuade Jennifer to sing at your high school reunion."

"You've got to be kidding," Abby laughed.

"No, I'm serious," Cassie said.

"What was the other message?"

"The second was from *People Magazine*. They

want to do a front cover with you and Jennifer called 'The Powerhouse Beauties.'"

Abby laughed. "That's hilarious."

Hearing his wife laugh, Brett Winterberg, the Head of the CIA, entered the room.

"Abby, what's so funny?"

"Ryan Rydell wants me to get Jennifer to sing at our thirtieth high school reunion, and *People* wants to put us on the cover, calling us 'The Powerhouse Beauties.'"

"But you are, my dear, you are," Brett teased.

"Well, this sweaty, stinky lady has got to get a bath before the State Dinner. I don't think the new Prime Minster of Spain would be too impressed with me now. I can see it tonight on the news. 'President Winterberg soils Vera Wang dress and offends Spain's Prime Minister with her horrible B.O. News at 11.' Hon, I'll meet you in the rotunda at 7:00," Abby said as she flew off for their living quarters.

"As you can see, I'm ready to escort you, my lady; even when you stink, you are still the most beautiful woman I've ever laid eyes on." Dressed in a striped tuxedo with flowing tails, which accentuated his dark features and his six-foot, muscular frame, Brett blew her a kiss.

"See you there, you handsome hunk, man of my dreams," Abby called out.

"Oh, you guys are so sickening sweet," Cassie said. "Brett, has Abby always been so pretty and kind?"

"Cassie, she has, but I bet you don't know why she was laughing about Ryan Rydell and *People Magazine*, do you?"

"No clue," Cassie said.

"Well, since, I'm ready for the State dinner and Abby's not, I have some time to tell you the story if you want to hear it?"

"Absolutely," Cassie said.

"Okay, but what I tell you has to be confidential. I'm not sure Jennifer wants the world to know her story."

"What do you mean?" Cassie asked.

"I'm convinced Jennifer would've never gotten to the point in her career where she would win an Grammy for best new album, 'Celebrating Life,' if it hadn't been for Abby," Brett said.

"How's that?"

"Ryan Rydell, who just called about the high school reunion, did everything in his power while he was in middle school to torture Jennifer. To think he would have the nerve to call Abby to get her to persuade Jennifer to sing was what was cracking her up, as well as *People* calling them 'Powerhouse Beauties.'"

"But you said Abby was always pretty. You didn't say she was an ugly duckling who turned into a swan."

"Abby has always been a beauty from the time she was born, her mom said. Jennifer wasn't, however. In fact, Ryan named her 'The Bucktoothed Girl.'"

"How'd you find all this out?"

"I was getting ready to propose to Abby when we were in law school. I went over to her mom's house to get some pictures of her because I was going to do a 'This Is Your Life, Abby Legna' PowerPoint in our Criminal Law class. The end was going to say that 'Your Life, Abby, will not be complete unless you have me in the second half. Marry me, please.'"

"But how does Jennifer fit in?" Cassie asked.

"I found a picture of Jennifer and Abby together in her yearbook when Abby had been elected Student Body President. I wouldn't have known it was Jennifer if I hadn't seen the caption below."

"Why?"

"Because, as Ryan so cruelly pointed out to her, she had really buckteeth," Brett said.

"But she's gorgeous now."

"Yeah, but Abby can take some credit for that. When she arrived at Concord Middle School, no one knew that Jennifer could sing. They just mocked her teeth. Abby's mom told me the story, and if you want, I will tell you 'The Rest of the Story.'"

"*Please!*"

"Well, let's go back to the year 2007."

# THE NEW GIRL

Jennifer paced up and down the hallway of her steamy trailer. She listened for the Concord Middle School bus to arrive. She looked at her fingernails, bitten to the quick. She faced the mirror. *How wonderful it would be if I could see a different face looking back at me. Why don't I look like Hillary Duff or Lindsay Lohan? Life is definitely not fair.* She opened and closed her mouth over and over again, hoping she would find a way to hold her teeth in when her mouth closed. But, just like the other million times she had tried, it didn't happen. As she continued fretting about her less than attractive face, she knew her clothes weren't going to help her either. They were her sister Hannah's hand-me-downs, badly worn, though not in a cool way, like the Gap's pants or Aéropostale's.

She heard the dreaded bus tires screech as the bus driver opened the doors. She knew she had to go and face whatever might happen on the bus. She yelled a quick, "Bye, Mom," picked up her worn book bag, shut the door of their trailer, climbed slowly up the bus stairs, and peered up and down the aisle for a seat. No one moved over. Since she was the last stop, the only available seat was right behind the driver. Her brief glance up and down the aisles had given everyone a chance to check her out.

As she sat down behind the bus driver and the bus pulled off, she heard chattering and snickering behind her. It had been deathly quiet when she boarded the bus. Now, the volume rose decibels. She felt like she was in the middle of a football stadium, a roaring crowd cheering for its chosen team. She couldn't make out any of the conversation. Because Jennifer had no one to talk to, she tried to enjoy the scenery outside.

After a few minutes, Jennifer felt a tap on her back. She turned around to face a girl with a mischievous look on her face.

"Hey, we were wondering what your name is?"

"Jennifer."

She wished she could be happy that she was asked. Her intuition told her otherwise; the girl was not trying to be friendly but had another agenda in mind.

Bringing Jennifer back from her thoughts to the present reality, the girl blurted out, "And we also want to know where you came from?"

"We just moved here from West Virginia," Jennifer wasn't sure where this conversation was headed. Trying to get the conversation off of her,

Jennifer asked the girl behind her, "What's your name?"

"Gretchen," she smirked.

The whole bus erupted in laughter.

"Nice to meet you, Gretchen." Desperate to make a friend, Jennifer continued to hope this was a friendly overture. Once again, the bus exploded in laugher.

"Niiice to meet you, too, *Jen-e-fer.*"

Laughter erupted all over the bus again. Jennifer realized then that the whole episode had been to entertain the bus. "Gretchen" had enjoyed mocking Jennifer's Southern accent, embarrassing her in front of the others. Jennifer had taken her bait. She quickly turned away from "Gretchen," breathing several deep breaths as the bus pulled into the school parking lot.

She hoped someone would show her the way and help her around. But, as she got off the bus and the other students moved around her, as if she weren't there, she knew she was on her own. Various groups of students turned around as they ran up the school's stairs, high fiving each other, and laughing, calling out, "Have a *nii-ice* day, *Jen-e-fer* duh!"

*Welcome to Concord Middle School. How am I going to make it through the day? Why did we have to move here? My life stinks.*

# RYAN AND COMPANY

If Jennifer thought she had experienced the worst that day, the attacks had only begun. She sat in her first period class and waited for the teacher to enter. Several of the boys who had been on her bus talked loudly, so Jennifer would hear.

"Hey, did you get a good look at the new girl, '*Jen-e-fer?*'"

"Yeah, she hurt my eyes," one of the boys said.

"I have never seen someone so ugly. I mean, did you check out those buckteeth?"

"Yeah, man. She looks just like a beaver."

"That's a great name for her. '*Jen-e-fer* the Beaver.'"

The class roared.

Miss Wagner, their first period math teacher and coordinator for the Student Council, then entered and commanded their attention. Her long, curly, black hair flowed down the length of her back. Her erect posture made her seem dignified and worthy of attention. It didn't hurt her popularity, either, that she never made a student feel dumb when he didn't understand Algebra.

"Ryan, was that your voice I heard when I was walking down the hall?"

"Yeszzz," Ryan, rolled his eyes and mumbled.

Jennifer now knew the name of her first tormentor; she wondered what Miss Wagner was going to say and do next.

"Well, it sounded as if you were telling a joke? Was that the case?"

"Yeah."

"Then share it with me. I love a good joke."

"I can't, Miss Wagner. It's not appropriate," Ryan said.

"Well, if you can't tell it to me, then I know you'll be glad to stay after school with your good friend Seth and help me with Student Council work for an hour," she said, putting an end to the challenge.

Seth blurted out, "Why me, Miss Wagner?"

"Because I also heard your voice, Seth. Am I right, or do I need to poll the class?"

"No need. I'll be there after school...Crap!" he said only for Ryan to hear.

"Good. I thought you would see it my way. Okay, class, let's get down to business. I see we have a new student," Miss Wagner said as she walked around the room. Looking right at Jennifer, she said, "Could you tell us your name and a little about yourself?"

Jennifer heard a few muffled laughs, to which

Miss Wagner shot an evil-eye look, warning Ryan and Seth not to persist or else.

"My name is Jennifer Alley, and I just moved here from West Virginia."

"Tell us some more, Jennifer. Like what do you enjoy doing?"

"My very favorite thing in the world to do is sing."

"Well, that's great. We have a talent show each spring. You'll have to enter. We have great prizes."

Again, the sound of muffled laughter rippled through the back of the classroom.

Jennifer knew it was coming from Ryan and Seth; so did everyone else. Ryan whispered to Seth, "Well, you know how some people sing like a dog, I guess she sings like a beaver." Seth tried hard to smother his laughter at Ryan's put-down.

"Ryan and Seth, since you are finding everything so funny today, I'm sure you would enjoy helping me not only today after school, but tomorrow as well."

Ryan blurted out, "You're kidding, right?"

"Trust me, I'm not kidding. I suggest you don't argue with me about this or both of you will find yourselves in In-School Suspension the first day of school. Do I make myself clear, guys?"

"Yes, Miss Wagner," they said simultaneously.

"Okay, time for math," Miss Wagner commanded.

Without catching Miss Wagner's attention, Ryan slipped Seth a note telling him not to worry—he had a plan. He wrote that he would share the plan with Seth later. They were not going to let Jennifer get away with this. Yet, revenge would have to wait a little, the note said. Once Seth read it, he shot Ryan the thumbs up sign. Megan Stewart had seen the note. She wrote Ryan one telling him to count her group in as well. She knew Andrea, Brooke, and Ashlyn would be game for some fun, but not "Miss Goody Two Shoes," Abby.

Having gotten in trouble with Miss Wagner twice in one day, Ryan and Seth left Jennifer alone in the other classes. Since they had to stay after school, the bus ride home was quiet as well. Jennifer's stomach became queasy as she thought about facing them the next day. It felt like someone had gone in and tied her insides in knots. She feared Ryan and Seth were going to have more in store for her after being given two days of after-school detention.

When Jennifer got home, her mother knew by reading her face that something was wrong. "Jennifer, come here. What happened at school today?"

Jennifer went through her day play by play with her mom. After she finished, her mom asked, "Jen, do you remember that quote you read me last year from Eleanor Roosevelt?"

"Yes, ma'am."

"Well, say it to me."

"'No one can make you feel inferior without your permission,'" Jennifer recited.

"Good. Let's talk about this for a minute. Jennifer,

even Jesus was persecuted by people who misjudged Him, and He was perfect.

That being the case, you can bet us imperfect beings are going to get it from time to time. Your dad has said from the day you were born that you are going to make a great impact on the world. If you let these two small-minded boys, Ryan and Seth, make you bitter, it won't happen."

"Thanks, Mom." Jennifer gave her mom a big hug. Her mom squeezed her back with all the comfort she could muster.

Jennifer went back to the room she shared with Hannah. Her thoughts went to how tough her mom and dad's life had been compared to hers. Her paternal grandfather, Albert, had died of alcoholism when her dad was only twelve. Her dad, Judd, had to quit school and go to work in the textile mill in order to put food on the table. There he had met Jean, a local beauty. She had been orphaned at five when her parents were killed as missionaries in Bogotá, Columbia. Jean had been sent to live with her only living relative, her Aunt Kathy. However, Kathy soon found that a small child hampered her single lifestyle. She quickly put Jean in the Children of God Orphanage. Jean had to go to work, too, at twenty-one. The orphanage required all their children to leave when they turned "the legal age." Some good did come out of the situation, because Judd and Jean found true love for the first time. They made a commitment to be there for each other always and any children they might have.

Sixteen years into their marriage with two daughters to support, the textile mill closed its doors when it couldn't compete with overseas labor costs. Judd found himself without a way to provide for his family. He had been grateful, however, when his brother, Uncle Bud, called him and told him about a job in Perdue's chicken factory.

"It isn't glamorous work; the plant smells awful," Uncle Bud said, "but it pays pretty decent if you can put up with the stench."

Presented with this opportunity, the Alley family packed their belongings and found themselves in Concord, North Carolina, ready to start a new life.

To add to the embarrassment and shame Jennifer felt about her teeth, all the Alley family could afford to rent in Concord was a trailer in a section of town called "Tower Circle." Most of the inhabitants of Tower Circle were illegal immigrants whom the authorities left alone because they were willing to work in the chicken factory. Yards overflowed with garbage and broken down cars. Bullet holes through windows manifested themselves as a warning to beware of the potential for violence. Many Saturday nights found the local police canvassing the area due to parties that had gotten out of hand, causing fights to develop. One officer, Pete, told Judd he really needed to get his family out of "TC." Pete was afraid someone would get hurt when the fighting involved weapons. Jennifer's dad had been saving money to afford something better. Jennifer wondered how long it would take. Judd hated being there. The heavy partying reminded him of how his dad used to binge drink, blowing his paycheck. It was déjà vu. Jean, on the other hand, found some comfort there. With her Spanish background, she bonded with the women who had been through similar ordeals, having left home for the United States in hopes of a better life. She helped interpret and lead them through all the required paperwork necessary to enroll their children in school, knowing that soon the children would be able to interpret for their parents.

Overwhelmed by these stressful thoughts, Jennifer told herself to snap out of it. No, they didn't have a lot of stuff the world considered important. But, from what she had observed of other families, they were rich in love. Her dad had never raised his voice at any of his children. The worst thing he could ever do was give one of his children "the look." It would crush the offender, because it said, "I'm disappointed in you." Neither one of his girls wanted to disappoint her parents. Judd and Jean constantly encouraged their girls to study hard so they would be able to go to college to make something out of their lives, an opportunity they never had.

*Wouldn't it be so cool to make them proud of me and have one of their wishes turn out?* She vowed she would make it happen. She decided to try to get some rest so she could face Ryan and Seth the next day.

After tossing and turning all night, Jennifer felt exhausted. She dreaded another day of Ryan and Seth's bullying. She didn't feel she had the energy to face them, but she had no choice. She had to go to school. Otherwise, a truant officer would come to the Circle, shaming her family. As she dressed and prepared for school, she tried without success to think of quick comebacks that might get them to lighten up.

The dreaded moment arrived; the familiar bus tires screeched and the bus doors opened. Jennifer walked out of her trailer and entered with apprehension. The bus took off. It seemed everyone was lost in conversation. She hoped the ride would go smoothly. She overheard conversations about how Concord High's football team was going to eliminate A.L. Brown High School's team and give them a night they would never forget.

Before she got on the bus, Ryan and Seth, the "cool" guys, had been plotting how they were going to get Jennifer back. After about five minutes, they started yelling, "Hey, '*Jen-e-fer!*'"

*Maybe if I ignore them, they will quit calling my name.*

"Gretchen," whose real name was Megan, tapped Jennifer on the shoulder.

"Ryan and Seth really want to talk to you, Jennifer. And, since they are the most popular guys in seventh grade, I suggest you turn around."

*What harm could it do?*

She stalled for a moment while they continued to call out her name.

"Hey, '*Jen-e-fer*' turn around," they yelled out again.

Jennifer whipped around to see what they wanted. As soon as she did, Ryan and Seth bared their teeth and started making beaver motions with their lips and teeth.

"Hey, look. It's the Beaver Girl!"

Trying to fight back tears, Jennifer turned around, attempting to contain the emotional upheaval within her. Seeing Jennifer's hurt and enjoying it caused other boys and most of the girls to join in.

"Beaver, Beaver," they all chanted while imitating the motions of a beaver chewing.

"It's the Beaver Girl, Beaver Girl," they all laughed. "Why don't you do something about those darn teeth, Beaver girl? Have you registered them down at the courthouse as legal weapons?" Ryan and Seth loved every minute of Jennifer's torment. They knew they had everyone's attention. They liked how powerful they felt. It was better than being "high."

# MISS WAGNER

By the time the bus pulled up to school, Jennifer's sobbing had caused her eyes to swell and look puffy. When she entered her first period ten minutes tardy, Miss Wagner immediately observed her discomfort.

"Jennifer, what's wrong?"

"Nothing, Miss Wagner, nothing. I just have really bad allergies." There was no way she was going to rat on Ryan and Seth. She was smart enough to know that if she did, her torment would never end.

"Okay," Miss Wagner said, not buying her story. She had worked with middle school students long enough to know otherwise. However, she did not want to embarrass her emotionally fragile student further. She let it go for the moment.

"Why don't you go to the bathroom and wipe your eyes with a wet paper towel? I won't count you tardy."

"Thank you, Miss Wagner."

Miss Wagner was sure someone in her class knew what really had happened. "Do any of you know something that has happened to Jennifer that she's not sharing, like a death in the family or something?"

"No, Miss Wagner," they all said in unison, except for Abby Legna, who believed lying was wrong. She was far from perfect, but Abby felt it was always important to admit your mistakes and be honest.

"Okay," Miss Wagner said, still not buying it but also noticing that Abby was not saying anything. She bet Abby would come clean after class. She also knew that if she asked Abby right after class, everyone would come down on Abby and make her the next target. Not wanting that to happen, Miss Wagner decided to wait until after school when she knew she would see Abby in Student Council.

Meanwhile, Jennifer, as she was walking down the hall, realized she had no idea where the bathroom was on this wing. Looking all around and not paying attention, she crashed into Mr. Little, the school principal. He steadied himself and didn't fall. Jennifer breathed a sigh of relief knowing how close she had come to knocking him down.

"What are you doing out of class, young lady? Can I see your hall pass?" Mr. Little gently asked, remaining calm as he waited for Jennifer to regain her composure.

She told him what she was doing, showed him her hall pass, and then looked for Mr. Little to direct her the right way. He wrote a note to find out later from Miss Wagner why her student was sobbing out in the hallway.

Making her way to the bathroom after her embarrassing encounter with the principal, Jennifer moved inside, eager to be alone. To her dismay, she saw two girls inside who looked somewhat familiar from the bus. They were obviously in no hurry to get to class. Touching up their make-up and hair had been their central focus until they spotted Jennifer.

As Jennifer made her way into the stall, she heard one of the girls say to the other, "Man, oh man, they will let anybody into this school. Won't they, Andrea?"

"Not just anybody, Brooke, even *an-i-mals*, it seems,"

Andrea said.

"You mean beavers, don't you?" Brooke asked.

They both viciously laughed.

"Hey, we better get to class. I can't afford a demerit. You know it would blow my mom's image of me being perfect and all," Andrea said.

The two girls sauntered out, laughing. "Bye, Beaver Girl."

Brooke continued... "Watch your chops so you don't cut anybody else down in the hall like you did Mr. Little. We saw your little episode in the hallway, you loser. Don't they have bathrooms in West *Vir-gin-e-a?*"

"TTFN (Ta Ta for Now)," Andrea yelled.

Jennifer sobbed in the stall. She had no desire to return to the class mob squad that seemed to be going after her. Even though she hadn't been in the popular group at her old school in West Virginia, she had friends. At Concord Middle, she was beginning to believe that all the students here were into bullying for their kicks.

*Please, God*, she silently prayed, *I know that your Son took a worse beating than this for me; He also felt alone and scared. But you gave Him the strength He needed. Please do the same for me.* At that moment, a beautiful girl, whom Jennifer had seen on the bus, walked into the bathroom. She had noticed this same girl had been one of the few who hadn't participated in the earlier teasing Jennifer had gone through on the bus.

"Hey, Jennifer. I'm Abby. Miss Wagner sent me to check on you since you hadn't gotten back to class. Are you okay?" Abby smiled as she was asking. Behind her gorgeous blue eyes, miniature beams of light twinkled. The atmosphere in the bathroom immediately changed; the room seemed lighter, the air less heavy. Jennifer now felt calmer and stronger.

"Yeah, I'm okay. It's just so hard to leave friends you love and come to a new school where everyone seems determined to make your life miserable," Jennifer said.

"Yeah, it can be tough here sometimes, but not everyone here is as shallow as Ryan and Seth are. Until someone puts them in their place, they'll probably keep on messing with people. The good news is,

I believe, that someday someone will. Now, come on, and get them out of your head," Abby said.

Jennifer had to admit she almost believed Abby's encouragement. The day proceeded without further incident until the three p.m. dismissal. Both Jennifer and Miss Wagner, in their respective classrooms, breathed a sigh of relief. Jennifer, for her part, breathed relief because she knew Ryan and Seth would not be on the bus. Miss Wagner felt confident she was going to get to the bottom of Jennifer's situation. She hated to see anyone so injured. She made up her mind to do what she could to change Jennifer's status with her peers.

The bell rang; the students spewed from the classrooms for their buses or rides home. Miss Wagner rushed down to the cafeteria to get Ryan and Seth started on their work and to find Abby.

"Seth and Ryan, I want you to make posters for the upcoming Student Council election. Once you have made ten and I approve them, I want you to hang them around the school. Here are materials to start. I have some more things in my car I am going to get Abby to help me carry in. The rest of you work on counting out ballots for your homeroom and then put them in your teachers' boxes."

"All right," they said in unison, for they would do anything for Miss Wagner. She was the epitome of cool. She was beautiful, smart, and knew how to orchestrate fun for her students. Her Student Council events were the ones students looked forward to all year. Miss Wagner had surprised them all when she had gotten the local TV station to agree to film and broadcast the upcoming talent show on the local station. It seemed there wasn't anything Miss Wagner couldn't do. Even the president of the bank had given saving bonds of sizable amounts for the prizes. Of course, he hoped his generosity would lead to a date with Miss Wagner, which was doubtful. Miss Wagner was picky when it came to men. She didn't care how much money they made; how they treated people was what was important to her. Miss Wagner had seen him scream at a waitress when she was with friends at The Union Street Bistro. That awful experience confirmed her decision to stay far away from Don Morgan.

As the others got started on their work, Miss Wagner and Abby walked out to Miss Wagner's car.

"Abby..."

"Yes?"

"I noticed that you didn't respond when I asked what happened to Jennifer. Do you know something about that?"

"Yes," Abby said in a whisper, as if someone might overhear their conversation. "I didn't want to get it from Seth and Ryan."

"What do you mean about getting it from Seth and Ryan? What part do they play in this?"

"Well, you know how Jennifer has really buckteeth?"

"Yeah, so?"

"Well, Ryan and Seth have been calling her 'Beaver' on the bus and in your class since school started," Abby said, glancing around, making sure no one had overhead her.

"Oh, now I get it, Abby. I'm glad you shared that with me. Believe it or not, I was teased like Jennifer when I was in school!"

"*You?*"

"Yes, me. I was so skinny that kids walked around calling me 'Bony' and said when I took a shower and turned sideways, I would go down the drain. One boy, whose parents were friends with my parents, even wrote 'Bony' throughout my yearbook. This was before the days of models like Kate Moss. Christie Brinkley was the person all the girls aspired to be; she was not skinny. She was well proportioned, if you know what I mean."

"Yes, ma'am, I do," Abby laughed.

"And," Miss Wagner continued, "I thought my face really must be ugly because all the boys would never look at me or ask me out. All of them talked non-stop about wanting to go out with Sharon Dante. I could never understand why until I got to college. Unfortunately for her, I realized it wasn't her face they were checking out."

"When people in college told me I was pretty, I was shocked, because no one outside of my family had ever told me I was attractive. You can imagine my amazement when one of my college girlfriends sent my picture to Elite Modeling, and they called me to fly to New York for an interview. Six months later, I was on the cover of *Life Magazine* for an article they were doing on summer fun. It featured me in a bathing suit. Skinny me."

"My college boyfriend put the stills of my photo shoots on his wall. He would invite his football friends into his room to look at my pictures. They couldn't believe it was me. You know how they talk about airbrushing and make-up?"

"Yeah, I've read some about that."

"Well, let's put it this way. You're like modeling clay to the people who work on you. You provide the form and they sculpt you to look the way they want with make-up and hairstylists. I would look in the mirror sometimes and not believe it was me looking back. You can imagine my shock when I was home for the weekend, and I ran into Sharon Dante at the grocery store. She congratulated me on the *Life* cover. Only then did I take a good look at her and realize she was not pretty and never had been. Cute, yes, but not pretty," Miss Wagner sighed after sharing so much about her past.

"What I quickly learned is that you can be 'it' in one place and 'nothing' in another depending on who your audience is and what its values are. So now, Abby, can you see why I cheer for the underdog?"

"Yes, yes, ma'am," Abby said, amazed at all that Miss Wagner had shared. As Miss Wagner had been sharing about being so skinny and what the media can do to your looks, Abby felt a twinge of guilt. She wanted to be super skinny, but it seemed she could never get down to her desired size. After her dad had died, it had been difficult to eat. The weight just dropped off her. Many people commented on how different she looked. Abby interpreted their comments to mean she looked better. She didn't realize people were concerned. They wondered if she ever was going to recover from the shock of her dad's untimely death.

Recently, as her appetite returned, she vowed not to gain the lost weight back. *I'm powerless to do anything about my dad's death, but I can control my weight, and I'm gonna.* She had eaten so little for lunch that day, she felt like she was going to pass out at any minute. Her mind jumped from thought to thought with lightning speed. Focusing on Miss Wagner proved challenging. Miss Wagner's emphatic voice interrupted her train of weight-loss thoughts.

"I have been 'nothing' and I have been 'it.' Now, where I want to be is in the classroom where I might help those who are struggling like I was. I hope to help Jennifer. Can I count on your help as well?"

"Yes, you can, Miss Wagner."

"Well, I have a plan. You're still planning on running for President of Student Council, right?"

"Why?"

"Because I want Jennifer to be your campaign manager. Can you go for that?"

"I'm not sure," Abby shot back, "but you know Ryan is planning on running too."

"Yeah, I know, but I have an idea."

"Cool."

"Well, I can't fill you in quite yet, because I need to consult with some friends, but I will get back to you soon, okay? In the meantime, give the idea some thought. Talk to your mom and get back to me."

"Sure, Miss Wagner," Abby said as she high-fived her very cool teacher. Abby had confidence that Miss Wagner's plan would hurt neither her nor Jennifer, and it was sure to be exciting. She had to admit the idea of Jennifer being her campaign manager scared her. She really wanted to win, but something inside her made her feel like she could trust Miss Wagner. She couldn't wait to get her mom's input when she got home from school.

# MISS EARLY

After Student Council, Miss Wagner rushed to find her friend, Gretchen Early, the guidance counselor. Miss Early worked late most days, trying to get caught up on paperwork.

"Gretchen, I'm so glad you're in your office," Miss Wagner almost yelled. "I've got to talk to you."

"What's going on, Whitney?" Miss Early knew for Miss Wagner to ask for help, it had to be serious, because Miss Wagner handled everything so well herself, especially the students.

"Have you met the new seventh grade student, Jennifer, yet?"

"No, because I won't do classroom guidance until September. What's her story?" Miss Early asked.

"Well, she has really buckteeth, and I think she would be adorable without them, but her family can't afford oral surgery and the braces she would need. So, knowing that she is sensitive about her teeth, Ryan and Seth have made her their target."

"Great. That's all a new girl needs is to have Ryan and Seth after her."

"Yeah, you're right about that. What I wanted to know, Gretchen, is if I can bring her down to see you during first period tomorrow? She has my class then."

"Sure, that'd be great." Like Miss Wagner, she had a tender spot for the down-and-out kid.

"Okay, see you then," Miss Wagner said as she whirled out of Miss Early's office. "I knew you would help. And after you talk to her, I'll let you in on my little plan."

"I'm intrigued," Miss Early called out to Miss Wagner, already halfway down the hall.

The next day, keeping her vow, Miss Wagner brought Jennifer to Miss Early's office. Jennifer's eyes, once again swollen and red, let everyone know she had been crying. Before she entered Miss Early's office, Jennifer paused at the nameplate outside her door.

"Your first name is Gretchen, Miss Early?"

"Yes, I know that it's an unusual name. Being a middle schooler, you probably haven't heard it before."

"I heard it on the bus the other day," Jennifer said.

"You mean the students were talking about me using my first name?"

"No, not exactly."

Perplexed, Miss Early asked, "What do you mean?"

"Megan Stewart told me my first day on the bus that her name was Gretchen," Jennifer said. "Why would she do that?"

"Is that the day the teasing started?"

"Yes, ma'am."

"Well, I think I can guess the answer. It's because I teach a lot about being friendly. I bet Megan was using my name in a sarcastic way to get a rise out of the other students. She knew her treatment of you would horrify me."

"Oh, I get it now. Do you think you can help me get rid of this nightmare?"

Miss Early's heart ached for Jennifer. She could see why she was being teased. Even with her mouth closed, she still could see Jennifer's teeth protruding. Although her clothes appeared clean, they were threadbare from so many washings.

*I wouldn't want to relive the horrors of middle school for anything. I've got to help this child.*

To Jennifer's question, Miss Early said, "Yes, I do believe I can help, Jennifer. We're going to do a little exercise called 'Power and Puppet' to get you to see what is going on with the people on the bus."

"What I want you to do," Miss Early continued, "is to stand up and face me."

"Okay."

"I'm going to have the power the first time, Jennifer, and you are going to have it the second time. The first time you are going to be my puppet. What that means, Jennifer, is that every time I use my power word, you have to do as I say. Every time you hear the power word, you will flap your arms and move around in a circle like a chicken."

"Think you can do that, Jennifer?"

"Yeah, it sounds weird, but I think I can do it."

"The power word can't be an adjective. Do you know what an adjective is, Jennifer?"

"Yes, it describes, like beautiful, ugly, et cetera."

"Right. The power word is going to be a noun: a person, place, or thing. Every time I say the power word, which is going to be the word 'shoe,' you're going to flap your arms and move around in a circle one time as if you were a chicken. Got it, Jennifer?"

"Yes, ma'am, I do."

"Okay, let's get started," Miss Early said.

"I was running down the road the other day, when my right shoe" (Jennifer flapped) "hit the side of the pavement and went spiraling into the middle of the road. I thought, *How am I going to be able to run without my shoe?* (Jennifer flapped). I decided to run out to the road and retrieve my shoe. (Jennifer flapped). But before I could reach it, a car came bounding up over the hill and hit my shoe. (Jennifer flapped). I mean it flattened that shoe. (Jennifer flapped). I thought, *How can I run home without my shoe?* (Jennifer flapped). Well, I decided I would just have to make the best of it, and I began to hop home with just one shoe. (Jennifer flapped).

"Well, Jennifer, how did it feel to be a chicken?"

"Pretty silly, Miss Early."

"Yeah, bet it did."

"Now, let's switch places and you chose a power word and I will be the puppet. What is the power word going to be, Jennifer?"

"Teeth."

"Okay, I'm game. Let's go."

"Once upon a time there was an ugly girl who was born with ugly teeth. (Miss Early flapped). She went about her life with her ugly teeth (Miss Early flapped) until one day while walking on the beach, she discovered a magic bottle. Out of the bottle, a genie emerged and told the ugly girl with the ugly teeth (Miss Early flapped) to make three wishes.

"'Okay,' the girl said. 'My first wish is for my ugly teeth (Miss Early flapped) to turn into beautiful white teeth.' (Miss Early flapped).

'Your wish is granted, miss,' the genie said. 'For your second wish, miss?" he asked.

'I wish those boys who have made fun of me would turn into toads.'

'Your wish is granted.' Then, the genie asked, 'Now, for your last and final wish?'

'I wish that a recording executive would offer me a recording contract.'

'That is easily granted.'

'Here it is.' With that, he hands her the contract of her dreams. The end."

"Good job, Jennifer. Please sit down. Jennifer,

I don't have to be the Wizard of Oz to know that you're the girl in the story. You know, sometimes hard situations are turned around and end up like a fairy tale. Usually, changing one's life takes hard work. Let's talk about the 'Power and Puppet' activity. Do you see how it relates to real life?"

"To tell you the truth, not really, Miss Early."

"Okay, fair enough. Let's change the analogy. Think of tennis. If you were playing a match, what would you hope would happen?"

"That I would win."

"Well, what if I knew that you had a weak backhand? Do you think I would be compassionate and only hit forehands to you?"

"Of course not, you would want to win, so you would hit as many shots to my backhand as possible."

"What was the reason again?"

"Because you want to win."

"Exactly. So, let's look at the game of life. Which did you like being the most? The person with the power or the person who was the puppet?"

"The person with the power."

"Why?"

"Because it was funny to see an adult flap her arms when I said the power word."

"Which do you think most little kids would choose?"

"The puppet, because they probably like being silly."

"Exactly. Which do you think middle schoolers would say?"

"The person with the power."

"Yes, the majority choose the power. Why do you think that is?"

"Because middle schoolers like to feel in control and boss other people around."

"Right. So, looking at your story on the bus, who has the power?"

"The boys."

"And who is the puppet?"

"Me."

"Yes, so just like in the 'Power and Puppet' activity, each time the boys called you 'Beaver' and you got upset, they were using the power word and you were flapping. When you got upset, it entertained them. You were putting on a show for them.

"To Ryan and Seth, you looked silly and they were laughing, like you wanted to do when I was the chicken. And, in the tennis analogy, they were serving to your backhand and you were missing the shot. They ended up winning because they had the power over you. They were pulling your strings. You need to pull your own strings, Jennifer, and not allow yourself to be controlled by others."

"I know, Miss Early, but it's so hard. It hurts so badly," Jennifer said, the pain obvious in her voice.

"Jennifer, I know it hurts your feelings, and it would hurt mine. I would feel like crying, too, but that's just what the boys are expecting you to do, like missing your backhand shot. You have to figure out a way to control the situation or game yourself."

"In tennis, you would have to position yourself so that you could hit the majority of the balls with your forehand and only an occasional ball with your backhand. On the bus, you have to figure out a way to pull their strings before they have a chance to pull yours," Miss Early said.

"But how do I do that?"

"There are lots of strategies. I'll explain five and you can choose which one you feel will work for you. Obviously, ignoring them is not going to work because you are on the same bus; they're not going to leave you alone now that they feel like they are winning. I believe one of these five will help you. Here we go.

"Number one; ask the bullies a way off the subject question to get them sidetracked first. Like, 'What's our math homework tonight'?"

"Number two; agree with the insult. 'Yeah, my teeth really are big, ha ha.' Even though you are agreeing with them, it's on your terms, and they end up feeling defeated. You steal their thunder."

"Number three; give them a sarcastic comment, like, 'Gee that's the nicest thing anyone has ever said to me. Your mothers must be so proud'."

"Number four; give them a compliment, like, 'You did a great job in math yesterday. Keep up the good work'."

"Or, number five; return the challenge. For

example, you could say, 'Hey, what's wrong with beavers?'"

"Whatever you do, Jennifer, you need to look them in the eye and say whatever you decide assertively. Don't use a wishy-washy voice. Say it like you mean it. I want you to think about it overnight and be ready for the boys when you get on the bus tomorrow. Do you think you can do that?"

"Yes ma'am," Jennifer said, not convinced she could, but she wanted to please this new person in her life who had given her so much helpful advice. Jennifer felt Miss Early's genuine concern about her well-being. She could tell it was more than just a job for the guidance counselor. *Seems like maybe Miss Early had some personal experience with this bullying junk.*

"And, Jennifer, if you feel like crying, stuff those tears inside until you get in the building. If you feel like you have to cry, come into my office afterwards. Whatever you do, don't cry in front of Ryan and Seth. We don't want them winning anymore."

"I understand."

"One last thing, Jennifer."

"Yes?"

"Get a good night's sleep so you are ready to win the game. Are you cool with that?"

"Yes, I'm cool with it, Miss Early. Thank you for your help."

"It goes without saying, I want a full report."

"You've got it," Jennifer said.

"Okay then, see you tomorrow."

As Jennifer went onto her class, Miss Early prayed a quick prayer. "Please, God, let her have the courage and the wisdom she needs to face those boys tomorrow."

# TURNING THE TIDE

Jennifer went home; in her mind, she replayed over and over what Miss Early had taught her. After a long period of brainstorming, she came up with a plan.

The morning seemed to come quicker than normal, but Jennifer felt confident she was ready. The same familiar tires screeched outside her window as she took her time leaving the house. As she climbed onto the bus, she rehearsed again what she was going to do. She took some deep breaths.

Of course, Ryan and Seth were still licking their wounds from having to stay two days after school working on Student Council projects. They weren't going to let a chance for revenge pass them by.

As soon as Jennifer sat down, the familiar scene played out once again. Ryan and Seth began calling out her name for the whole bus's entertainment.

"*Jen-e-fer*, oh, *Jen-e-fer*, oh *Bee-ver!*" they taunted.

Jennifer quickly snapped her head around before

Zack and Seth could say or do anything. She made the motions of a beaver with her lips and teeth.

The bus erupted with laughter. But this time, they were laughing along with Jennifer, not at her. Ryan and Seth were speechless. They didn't know what to do next. They remained on the bus stunned.

Jennifer sure liked how it felt being the one who was pulling her strings, for a change. Several students high-fived her as they got off the bus. Jennifer stepped off slowly, relishing her victory, as a huge smile lit up her face. Ryan and Seth rushed by her a few minutes later, shouting, "You're such a loser, Beaver Girl," but it was obvious to everyone they were embarrassed.

When Abby made her way off the bus, she ran up to Jennifer and said, "Way to go, Jennifer. Hey, by the way, please sit with me and my friends at lunch today. We always take the blue table. Is that cool with you?" Abby waited for an answer.

"Sure," Jennifer said. "See you then."

Both girls took off for class. At lunchtime, Abby rushed to her group's regular table. She wanted to forewarn her group that Jennifer would be sitting with them because she knew it might be a problem with some of the girls.

Ashlyn fired off first, "Oooh, she is so ugly and so totally uncool, Abby. You can't be serious about her hanging out with us. What will people say about *us* if we are seen hanging out with her?"

"Yeah and she's so geeky too. I don't want to hang out with such a dorkus," Andrea added.

"Come on, girls," Abby begged. "Have'ya never read the stories of famous models who said they were ugly ducklings growing up? You never know what Jennifer may be when she grows up. She may be famous and look back and thank us for being her friends."

"Yeah right, Abby," Andrea whined. "But since you are so sweet, we'll be cool with it, right girls? We'll all be humiliated together."

"Right!" they all said together. Though the girls in the group had done some mean things when Abby was not around, they were completely loyal to her, all except Megan, who flitted back and forth from their group to another. Everyone had long figured out that Megan was jealous of Abby. When Abby was around, the group listened to her and not to Megan. Megan couldn't stand that. It also made her resentful; when one of them had a birthday, the birthday girl would find her favorite candy in her desk, secretly planted by Abby. Or, if one of them were having a bad day, she would find an encouraging note taped to locker—again from Abby.

When her father, Chet, had died was the only time they had ever seen Abby "down." For weeks she walked around looking sleep-deprived. The truth was she hadn't slept through the night for several weeks straight. To give her some relief, her doctor had prescribed a sleep aid for her to use during this tough phase. Since she had been there for her friends so many times and still wasn't one hundred percent, they would do whatever they could to show her support. They were anxious for the old Abby to return. She had been "mopey" and "down" for too long.

"Good, because here she comes," Abby said. "Jennifer, over here!" Abby yelled out.

"Hey, y'all," Jennifer said, checking out the girls' faces for their reactions.

"Jennifer, this is Andrea, Ashlyn, Jacqueline, Brooke, and Lauren."

Brooke and Andrea looked at her with threatening eyes, letting Jennifer know she'd better not comment on what had taken place in the bathroom earlier that week.

"Nice to meet you," Jennifer said. She had no intention of reliving what had happened in the bathroom. If hanging with Abby meant putting up with Brooke and Andrea, she felt pretty sure she could do it. Having Abby as an ally would help her ignore their standoffishness.

A few minutes later, after Jennifer had sat down, Rosalie, her neighbor in Tower Circle, passed by.

"Hola, Jen (Hello, Jen)," Rosalie said.

"Hola, Rosalie. (Hello, Rosalie.) ¿Quiere sentarse? (Do you want to sit down?)"Jennifer said.

"No, gracias, (No, thank you.) Estoy buscando a mi novio, Fernando. Vamos a estudiar el inglés antes del examen (I'm looking for my boyfriend, Fernando.

We're going to study our English before out test this afternoon)," Rosalie said.

"¡Bueno, y buena suerte¡ (Okay then, and good luck!)" Jennifer responded as Rosalie waved back.

Before anyone else could speak, Lauren blurted out, "Jen, you speak Spanish?"

"Yeah," Jennifer said, not sure if this was going to be a good thing or bad.

"Are you Spanish?" Andrea said with a glance around to her clique implying that a 'yes' answer would confirm that Jennifer, indeed, was the loser they thought she was.

"No, my mom was a missionary kid in South America. Her parents were massacred in front of her when she was five years old. She was then sent to the States, but thankfully she was able to remember her Spanish. She has raised Hannah, my sister, and me to be bilingual. I have to say knowing Spanish has come in very handy in many different situations. I'm glad my mom made me learn it."

"That's so cool," Lauren said. "I want to learn another language. I think it would be awesome to know what someone else was saying when they were speaking Spanish or French or even Italian. Don't you guys?"

"Yeah, right, Lauren, whatever you say," Ashlyn said. The conversation shifted to the latest movies. But, in all the girls' opinions, except for Andrea and Brooke's, Jennifer's level of coolness had moved up a notch.

Andrea's and Brooke's moms had taught them to believe that people who lived in trailers were somehow sub-human. Not thinking for themselves, they had accepted this. However, when Andrea had found out that Jennifer lived in a trailer, she thought back to her best friend in the third grade, Toni Tadlock. She had cried so hard when her mom had told her she couldn't sleep over at Toni's because, "You know," her mom said, "Toni lives in, you know, yuck, in one of those trailers on Tower Circle. You might get lice."

To which Andrea had questioned, "So?"

"Andrea Marie Zimmerman, you know that you are better than *those people*," her mom said, oozing with contempt.

It had broken Andrea's heart when Toni and her family left in the spring to pick apples in the mountains. Andrea's mom, on the other hand, had been thrilled.

*I wonder how Toni is doing...if she thinks about me ever.* Andrea dismissed the thought, because just as her mom had hoped, Andrea Marie Zimmerman now believed she was truly better than *those people*.

After a long discussion about Lindsey Lohan's latest movie, Ashlyn brought up the subject of the Student Council election.

"You are running for president, aren't you, Abby?" Ashlyn said.

"Yep."

"Do you really think you can beat Ryan?" Ashlyn said.

"We'll soon see, won't we?"

"Who's going to be your campaign manager?" Brooke said.

"Well, I was planning on asking Joy, but you guys know she's not starting back this fall while she is fighting her cancer and getting treatments. Miss Wagner is going to her house to tutor her once a week, she told me, and then Joy's mom is trying to do the rest."

"Yeah, it's so sad," Brooke said while the others shook their heads in agreement. "So, if not Joy, who then?"

"Well, I haven't had a chance to ask her yet, but I was planning on asking Jennifer."

"Jennifer?" They all yelled out, for no one entered their clique without the group's agreement. With Joy home sick, Jennifer replacing her didn't fit their way of thinking. They had a "cool" image to keep up. They were the blonde beauties of the school, who often dressed alike and were always in agreement about the important things in life. "Beaver Girl" was way off the "cool" radar, in the realm of nauseating and disgusting.

"Yeah, I like the idea of the new kid on the block. Nothing like putting you on the spot. Whadd'ya say, Jennifer?"

"I don't know," Jennifer hesitated in saying any

more. *If I am Abby's campaign manager, Abby is bound to lose. We'd probably be laughed off the stage.*

"Well, I'm not going to take 'No' for an answer unless you're in the hospital the day of the election. So it's settled. I'll see you today after school in Miss Wagner's room to begin working, if you can make it."

Jennifer had never known someone so sure of herself and what she wanted, yet not stuck-up about it.

"Sure, I'll be there if Miss Wagner can give me a ride home."

"Oh, I'm sure she can."

Feeling a little pleasure at the girls' stunned reactions and Abby's determination to hold firm to her choice, Jennifer smiled as the bell rang, directing them to fifth period.

Later that afternoon, Abby hustled down to Miss Wagner's room ahead of Jennifer and relayed to her teacher what had happened at lunch.

"You should have seen their faces, Miss Wagner. Brooke, Andrea, and Ashlyn sat there like I was out of my mind. Lauren and Jaqueline thought it was cool. But I'm sure Brooke, Andrea, and Ashlyn are *I-Ming* with Megan right now, saying that I've really lost it this time," Abby laughed.

"Are you sure you're okay with this plan of mine?"

"I prayed about it; I feel like there's something bigger going on here than just a Student Council election. My mom can assure you that I never do anything I don't want to do. We talked about it for a long time. We both agree if my dad were alive, he would say, 'Do it, Abby. Trust Miss Wagner on this one'."

Abby and Miss Wagner, hearing footsteps, looked towards the door as Jennifer walked in. The conversation shifted to planning Jennifer and Abby's speeches. Miss Wagner had to go over public speaking techniques with Jennifer, who had no experience. Afterwards, Miss Wagner took both girls home. She had been to the Legnas' before Abby's dad had died. She had taught Brandon, Abby's older brother, and had been at one of the parties celebrating Chet's election as senator. The Legna house was one of the prettiest on Union Street. It was a two-story Victorian house with a wraparound porch. The previous owners had been the Brown Family, who owned the textile mills in Concord and even the one in West Virginia where Judd had worked. Each room in the house had a theme based on world travels the Legnas had taken. Miss Wagner's favorite was the African room with the wicker ceiling fans, bamboo chairs, wooden carved animals almost six feet tall, multiple flowing fountains, and various flora the Legnas had been able to bring through customs to their home.

However, Miss Wagner had never driven on Tower Circle. She was embarrassed to admit it, but she felt nervous. When Jennifer asked her to come inside, she momentarily paused while trying to think up an excuse about some work she needed to do, but her conscience wouldn't let her lie.

As they entered the trailer—a first for Miss Wagner—Jennifer's mom greeted them. Miss Wagner couldn't get over noticing how beautiful Jean was. She towered almost six feet tall with brunette hair, graying, as though she had gone to a beauty salon to have her hair highlighted. The only hair salon Jean had ever been in, however, was the one she cleaned by the mall every Saturday night. Jean's natural highlights gave her a striking salt and pepper look. To add to her beauty, her skin was a deep olive color, which gave the illusion of a year-round tan.

Miss Wagner had noticed the beautiful garden as she entered. Jennifer informed her it was her mom's exclusive domain. She explained to Miss Wagner that Jean's parents had grown a garden they lived off in Columbia. Jean retained the knowledge of planting during the correct seasons. When one season ended, Jean canned and froze those items until the next season; year round their freezers were full. They ate as well as anyone in the county. Jean was also notorious for giving to friends from her bounty. Miss Wagner had the feeling she would not go home empty-handed.

"Miss Wagner, it's so nice to finally meet you. Thank you for helping Jennifer adjust to her new school and bringing her home. Please sit down," Jean said, warmth radiating from her.

Meanwhile, Hannah emerged from her room and headed to the kitchen. She called out asking if they would all like some ice cream. Everyone nodded enthusiastically, as that particular day had been a scorcher. As Hannah was scooping ice cream, Judd walked in from work. He told Hannah he would love some as well.

When Hannah brought their ice cream to them in the den, Miss Wagner noticed everyone was eating out of a bowl except Hannah. She thought it odd that Hannah ate out of a coffee filter. Judd put a chicken from work in the freezer. Then, he, too, walked over to Miss Wagner in the den, thanking her for helping Jennifer and for bringing her home. Miss Wagner couldn't help noticing his clothes held that familiar awful odor she smelled when she drove by the Perdue factory. It appeared his family had acclimated to it. She smelled a whiff of it when she entered the trailer. She thought there was probably nothing they could do to rid themselves of it. Over time, it appeared they had become oblivious to it.

As she was preparing to leave, Jean, true to her reputation as a giver, handed Miss Wagner a grocery bag loaded down with fresh vegetables and fruits from her garden.

"Do you think you'll be able to use these, Miss Wagner?"

"Absolutely. This will save me a trip to the Home

Economist. I hate eating anything canned because of all the preservatives they put in things today. I only buy fresh stuff. Thank you so much, Mrs. Alley," she said. Miss Wagner felt a twinge of guilt in taking from them when they had so little, but she knew if she refused the offer, they would have been offended and hurt.

Driving home, thinking how generous the Alleys had been with the little they had in the world and how selfish most people were, Miss Wagner realized why Hannah had been eating out of a coffee filter. Hannah had been taught to put other people before herself. There were four of them; Miss Wagner made an extra person. Hannah wouldn't have her guest be the one without the bowl. She had graciously made a makeshift bowl for herself out of the coffee filter.

Tears welled up in Miss Wagner's eyes.

"Lord, help me be more appreciative of what I have and more of a giver like the Alleys. And, bless them Lord, for their generosity. Thank you for what they have just taught me about what is really important."

She continued driving home as the tears rolled down her face.

# THE STUDENT COUNCIL ELECTION

The air in the auditorium was festive. There was lots of laughter and even an occasional bet about who was going to win. Everyone knew that this year's election was going to be close. Ryan was popular, but Abby was smart, well liked, and beautiful. Seth and Jennifer were the campaign managers. Miss Wagner drew from a hat and determined Seth and Ryan would go first.

"Hi, everybody! How y'all feeling today? Well, I'm feeling fine, and I want you to know that I have the people's candidate right here. My candidate has lettered in every sport and is the captain of the football team! (Eliciting whoops from the audience). And, most amazingly of all, he can bench press 150 pounds, which is pretty awesome for his size. And, now, without furthering waiting, I give you the people's candidate, Ryan Rydell," Seth said, certain of a sure rout.

"Well, guys, you know we all work hard and need a break from time to time. I promise you that when

I am elected, I will give us an hour off on Friday afternoon once a month to play Intramurals. You can count on me to be your man and take care of you!" (Eliciting more whoops). Ryan, full of cockiness, exited the stage, strutting for all he was worth, flashing the victory sign.

"That's it?" Miss Wagner said.

"Yes, ma'am. I'm such a shoo in, I didn't want to rub Abby's nose in her overwhelming defeat," Ryan said.

Abby rolled her eyes, listening to what Ryan was saying, while waiting backstage with Jennifer for her turn. She did think, however, that Ryan looked extraordinarily good-looking that day. He had just gotten his dark brown, spiked hair tinted with blond streaks, which made his deep brown eyes stand out even more. He was dressed in a killer outfit from Abercrombie and Fitch; all his years of weight lifting had "ripped" his arms and chest. It seemed to Abby as if Ryan had just stepped off the cover of a *GQ Magazine* to appear at Concord Middle for a moment. He literally took her breath away. Miss Wagner's announcement brought Abby back to reality.

"Our next candidate is Abby Legna, and introducing her will be Jennifer Alley."

Muffled snickers were heard throughout the auditorium. Mr. Little, the principal, held his hand up for silence. "Show some respect, people, or you all will have detention," he said.

The audience quieted down.

Jennifer began to speak, "As a newcomer, you are looking for that friendly face when you enter a school—someone who is kind and open to all types of people. Someone who you know will not judge you but who will seek to encourage you, knowing how hard it is to start over at our age in an unfamiliar place. Abby was that person for me. Her campaign goal is to make this a kinder place, so that anyone walking in will find acceptance. This is her way of honoring her dad, who, as most of you know, was tragically killed six months ago. I was sent this poem in an e-mail by an anonymous author, which I believe applies to Abby.

"'*God blesses us with people who brighten up our days by taking the time to listen and to care. They really make a difference with their kind and helpful ways. They see our needs and they lift us up in prayer.*

"*God blesses us with people who always make us smile. They share our happy moments and our tears. Their gentle ways of giving make living more worthwhile. They only grow more special through the years.*'

"Please welcome the candidate who can bring lasting change—not just to our activities, but to our hearts—Abby Legna."

Jennifer walked off the stage and gave Abby a huge hug as she exited.

"Thank you, Jennifer, for such a nice introduction. I don't think I am worthy of all that, but I do feel honored. Hello, Student Body. Yes, my name is Abby Legna and my campaign is about kindness. Most of you know that my dad was one of our senators from North Carolina in the United States Senate. He was killed in an airplane crash as he was coming home early in a private small airplane to see my last soccer game. As everyone I'm sure knows, he never made it. At his funeral were lots of famous people, including the president, but the person most of the people there remember was my grandfather. 'Pa,' as I call him, was immensely proud of my dad and all his accomplishments. He was always preaching to my dad and us that the only legacy you leave behind is the impact you have had on other people. He read this poem at my dad's funeral, which made many people cry. It's called '10 Things God Doesn't Care About,' and as he read it, he substituted in my dad's name.

### "'TEN THINGS GOD WON'T ASK YOU, CHET, WHEN YOU MEET HIM TODAY IN HEAVEN.'

1. Chet, God won't ask what kind of car you drove. He'll ask how many people you drove who didn't have transportation.
2. God won't ask the square footage of your house. He'll ask how many people you welcomed into your home.
3. He won't ask about the clothes you had in your closet. He'll ask how many you helped to clothe.
4. God won't ask what your highest salary was. He'll

ask if you compromised your character to obtain it.

5. He won't ask what your job title was. He'll ask if you performed your job to the best of your ability.

6. God won't ask how many friends you had. He'll ask how many people to whom you were a friend.

7. He won't ask in what neighborhood you lived. He'll ask how you treated your neighbors.

8. God won't ask about the color of your skin. He'll ask about the intentions of your heart.

9. He won't ask why it took you so long to seek Salvation. He'll lovingly take you to your mansion in heaven and not to the gates of hell.

10. And, Chet, He won't ask you if you loved Him, because He knows that you do. He will give you your crown and embrace you and say, 'Well done, my good and faithful servant. May your family and friends see your legacy of the countless ways you honored Me and may they be challenged to follow your lead. Your kindness will not go unnoticed.'[1]

"Guys, since that day, I have chosen to do whatever I can to respect everyone I encounter. I believe we all have value and that there is a plan and purpose for every life. Of course, some people make bad choices, and some do horrible things, but I believe strongly that we were all created with great worth. It is wrong to feel like you are less than anyone else, because that says the Creator made a mistake. But to say that you are better than someone else says the

Creator has favorites. That's not the case. I want us to be a school that stands out. When people walk in, I want them to sense something different about the teachers and the students. I want that to be kindness. Help me honor my dad by starting me on my path in government, where I can try to be a shining light like he was." Abby then walked off the stage.

For a few seconds, complete silence reigned, followed by loud noises—not whooping. The entire Student Body wept together, sighing and sniffling. Ryan felt nauseated because he knew Abby had the election in the bag. The majority of people in town admired Chet Legna; even those with a different party affiliation respected him. While Chet was alive, he was well-loved; now that he was dead, he was almost a saint; most of the town felt sorry for Abby, knowing he had been killed coming to watch Concord Middle's girls' soccer match. Ryan realized his peers would start Abby on her path in politics as a way to honor her dad and make sense of the tragedy.

He thought of how his dad, on the other hand, was so different. Ryan's dad just cared about getting the latest Jaguar or Lexus. When his dad found out about him, Seth, Brooke, Andrea, and Ashlyn egging Jennifer's trailer while her parents were out, Mr. Rydell laughed. The next morning, Jennifer's dad had called Ryan's dad on the phone and demanded that Ryan come over and clean up the mess. While her parents were at the grocery store, Jennifer had witnessed the egging from her bedroom, Mr. Rydell explained. She thought, at first, that people were shooting at the house, but even when she could see clearly that they were using eggs, not bullets, it still was devastating. Mr. Rydell hung up on Mr. Alley in mid sentence without apologizing for Ryan's antics. Later that afternoon, on their way home from school, Mr. Rydell and Ryan drove by Jennifer's trailer. They saw Abby and her mom out with buckets of water and sponges thoroughly cleaning all the windows. The night of the egging Ryan had laughed about what he and his friends were doing. Now he was feeling a little guilty. The image of Jennifer's hurt face peering through the window tormented his conscience.

As for the rest of his egging buddies, Seth stared at the floor as Abby spoke. Andrea, Ashlyn, and Brooke were searching for mirrors to fix their raccoon look due to their mascara running. Even though they could be mean as snakes, they did have a conscience, and Abby had touched their hearts in her speech.

Megan was seething in jealousy, knowing that Abby would be the president. Every time they would have an assembly, she was going to have to look at her onstage. She thought if she were at any other school without Abby Legna, it would be her on the stage as president. She consoled herself with the fact at least Ryan liked her and not Abby. He was the best-looking guy at school. At least she had something Abby didn't. Megan imagined herself twenty years in the future as Mrs. Ryan Rydell and Abby as an old maid. That caused her to laugh aloud. When she did, the other students shot her a look, asking, "What's up with you?"

After a few minutes of sobbing throughout the auditorium, the afternoon sun reached its zenith for the day, burst through the room, and bathed everyone in light. No one said anything. Finally, Mr. Little ended the moment of enlightenment for many by announcing the bell would ring in three minutes for dismissal, so the students needed to get ready to go home.

No one was shocked when Abby won the presidency. Unbeknownst to the rest of the Student Body, she received a call congratulating her from another president. This one lived in Washington and had made a point of keeping tabs on her because her dad had been a spiritual advisor to him.

Mr. Legna had prayed frequently with the president when the president was faced with overwhelming decisions. What the president said to her that night had a huge impact on the rest of her life.

"Abby," her mom called out to her that night as she was studying. "You have an important phone call."

"I'll be right there, Mom." Abby padded down the hallway to the kitchen in her flip-flops and pajamas. She couldn't imagine who would be calling this late. "Who is it, Mom?"

"Why don't you pick up and find out?"

"Okay," now very curious. "Hello?"

"Hello, Abby. This is the president. How are you doing? I hear congratulations are due."

"Hello, Mr. President. Thank you very much. How did you know?"

"Your mom called my office and told my assistant, Luisa Sanchez. I had asked your mom at your dad's funeral to call me anytime something major happened in your life. She thought this qualified. So do I."

"Thank you so much. This is such an honor."

"Abby, while I have you on the phone and I have a minute, I know it is late, but I just got Luisa's message. I had been in a meeting about more funding for schools. I want you to know about the last conversation I had with your dad, if you want to hear it."

"Of course."

"Good, I think you will enjoy this story. Your dad had come to a State Dinner honoring the new Prime Minister of Spain, Mr. Zapetera. Your brother, Brandon, had come with him because your mom was with you at a debate tournament."

"Yes, I remember that," Abby said. "Brandon really had fun."

"Well, after the dinner, I asked your dad and Brandon if they would come back to my office. I was really distressed about the events in the Middle East; I wanted your dad to pray with me concerning decisions I was going to have to make. After the serious part of our time was over, I started some small talk with Brandon about whether or not he was going into politics like his dad."

Abby laughed. "Brandon, no way."

"Yes, that's exactly what he said. When I questioned him to find out why not, he said he had gotten turned off watching all the negative ads about his dad and seeing how mean people could be when his dad was giving speeches," the president said.

"Yeah...I was just a little girl when dad started campaigning, but I have heard the stories."

"Then you know the one about you then, don't you?"

"Yes, my dad never tired of telling it," Abby laughed. "He thought it was hilarious when I was asked by a CNN reporter if I wanted to grow up and be a senator from North Carolina, and I said, 'No way, I am going to be the first woman president.'"

The president chuckled. "Abby, you know what your dad said to me that night? After Brandon shared his plans to bike race professionally and hopefully compete in the *Tour de France*, your dad said you would be the one to go into politics. He was almost sure of it. He said to me, 'Mr. President, you have never seen a child that people so easily relate to. Old people, young people...everybody,' he said. 'And she is so smart and articulate,' your dad added."

"Oh, that's so sweet. Thank you, Mr. President, for sharing that with me." Abby felt a warmth swelling in her heart, one she had lacked for months. *Welcome back to the land of the living.*

"It's my pleasure. I want you to know that I am here for you any time you need anything. You just call my office and Mrs. Sanchez will get the message to me. I'm pulling for you too. Your dad was a great man and a great friend. Abby, I feel sure you will continue his work for this great nation. My prayers are with you and your family. Take care, Abby."

"I will, Mr. President. Thank you for calling," Abby said and hung up. In her heart, she was determined to accomplish what her dad and the president had predicted would happen. It was the only way she could have peace about her dad's death. She had wrestled with guilt for so long knowing that her dad had been on his way home to see her soccer match. *What if he had just gone onto his scheduled meeting? He would still be here!*

On top of that, she felt so odd being fatherless. It wasn't fair for her dad not to be around when she needed him so much. Every day when she came home from school, she hoped in secret she would find out it had just been a bad dream; she would wake up and find her dad in front of her again. But the reality was always the same. He wasn't there. She felt as if she had an appendage removed and was walking around as an amputee. In addition, she couldn't understand why God would allow this to happen when she was so young. She confessed she didn't understand "why?" and was sometimes very angry about the situation. If life were a game, she thought, like the cliché goes, then she had been cheated in a major way.

However, she did have a peace that she would be reunited with her dad in heaven one day. Moreover, she had gotten a sense of relief when she prayed, even as her heart was bursting with grief, that her dad would give her some sign he was okay and that everything she believed was true.

Matching the atmosphere inside the Legna home, the morning of the funeral it was raining blinding sheets. When Abby got up to read her Scriptures at the podium, the rain continued to pelt; as she finished, it abruptly halted. Walking back to her seat through her tears, she saw a rainbow beaming its broad colors outside through the windows of the church directly to where she had been sitting, welcoming her with its beauty. *There's my sign. Thank you, God. I get it.*

Abby's thoughts were interrupted as she saw her mom crying; she realized she knew why. Her mom had been thinking the same thing she had. They were both missing her dad. She knew her mom needed her mood lightened; she ran up to her, flung her arms around her, and said, "Mom, that was *soooo* cool the president called. Thank you for the surprise."

"You're welcome, sweetheart! What did he say, sweetie?" Abby knew her mom was putting on the mom face, pushing her own sad thoughts aside.

After sharing the president's exciting conversation, Abby went to bed and slept straight through the night for the first time since her dad had died.

Back at school, to Abby's credit, she went with Ryan's plan for monthly Friday afternoon Intramurals, which she assigned him to coordinate. A week after the election, Abby had Ryan meet her after school in the gym to plan. She was a little nervous about meeting with him, not knowing how he was handling his defeat, but also because Abby knew about the egging. As usual, Abby greeted him in her normal way, being kind and friendly. She nervously made small talk, hoping that Ryan wouldn't hear her stomach churning, spewing its acids around as a result of her decision to skip lunch again. Her mom had forced her to go for a physical the day before. The doctor's diagnosis bothered her. Dr. Weston said she was severely depressed and needed to continue her antidepressant treatment.

*How long am I going to stay depressed? Who wouldn't be depressed after losing their dad? Are you supposed to just 'snap out of it?' That seems cold, not to be bothered by losing a loved one. Hey, another time and place for these worries. I've got to deal with Ryan now and be cool about everything.*

"Hey, Ryan, I can't wait to hear your great ideas for Intramurals. I know all the students are looking forward to the fun you have in store for them."

"Hey, Abby. Congratulations on the election. You'll be a prettier president than I would've been."

"Thanks, Ryan," she laughed.

"Hey, listen, I saw you over at Jennifer's cleaning up what we did. You could've gone to the administration and gotten me kicked out of the election before it even began. Why didn't you?"

"Ryan, my parents grilled me since I was a little girl that life is a gift. We don't have time to waste. Boy, do I ever know that after losing my dad. I wasn't ready to be fatherless. My mom was held at gunpoint when she was a teenager. I have learned from both of them that life is fragile," Abby said.

"But you didn't make the mess, so why were you cleaning it up?"

"Though I said I am fatherless, I am not Fatherless," Abby said.

"Huh? What are you talking about?" Ryan asked, bewildered.

"My earthly father is not here, but my heavenly one always is. If I thought I would never see my dad again, I would truly despair. But my heavenly Father gives me the strength to get through each day and, until recently, some heavy-duty medication from my doctor."

Ryan laughed. "I still don't get what you were doing over at Jennifer's?"

"Jennifer needed us. I may not go around with a Bible, broadcasting that I am a Christian. I have always thought if people couldn't tell you were by your actions, you must be missing the mark somehow. I know that I'm going to heaven; I don't have to earn that right. However, I am expected to use my days and gifts to make an impact for good. I believe I will give an account one day as to the decisions I have made.

"Just like Jesus said that when you give another water, you are doing it unto him; well, helping Jennifer was my way to honor not only her, but also my Lord. My mom was with me for the same reason."

"I guess you guys were really mad at me. Why were you still friendly?"

"Ryan, *mad* wouldn't be the right word. Disappointed, maybe. Until a person learns that life is fragile, it's easy to take it for granted and not realize that we're all valuable, God-created. I hurt for Jennifer, Ryan, but I think the Lord gave her the strength to forgive you. I'm sure she'll probably never forget the things you've done to her, but she's definitely a stronger person as a result of the things you have put her through."

"Wow, I never thought about it like that before," Ryan said, hanging his head. "You've given me a lot to think about. But, to be honest, this is getting too deep for me right now, and I would really like to get back on track planning the Intramurals. Is that cool?"

"Sure, Ryan," Abby said, as she put her hand on his shoulder. "By the way, you're welcome at my church anytime. I'll save you a seat if you'll come. We really have fun at my church. It's probably very different from anything you've ever experienced. We're all happy to be there. The atmosphere is usually electrifying."

"Fun, in church? That doesn't sound possible. Maybe, Abby, one day. Maybe one day."

"Just know that none of us are promised tomorrow."

"Then I wouldn't have to worry about next week's exams, now would I?"

They both laughed, realizing the tension had lessened between the two of them; they were able to return to the task before them.

*Man, if Miss Wagner weren't so beautiful, I would hate her. I can't believe that of all the people in the class, she would pair me up with Jennifer on purpose, to torture me some more. But if I don't want to fail her class, I've got to call 'Beaver Girl.'*

"Hello?"

"May, I speak to Jennifer, please?"

"Who's calling?"

"Ryan Rydell."

Long pause. *Great, now I'm going to get it.*

"Just a minute," he heard as the phone banged the counter, slammed down on its receiver.

After what seemed like forever, Jennifer picked up.

"Ryan?"

"Yeah, it's me. We gotta work on this math project. You ready to chunk the numbers for the math game?"

"Sure. How did the basketball game go?"

"It was okay."

"What was the score?"

"One hundred to seventy-five. We won."

"How many did you score?"

"Me? Forty-five, I think."

"Wow, your parents must be really proud."

Long pause.

"Ryan?"

"Yeah, I'm here."

"You sound down. I don't get why."

"It's just..." before Ryan knew what he was doing, he began unloading what had happened at the game. Ryan had been flying high from his performance, dancing around the locker room until his dad came in. The atmosphere in the locker room quickly changed when his dad entered, he explained. His dad let everyone know he was upset. The colors of his face beat bright red; the veins in his neck looked as if they might pop out. All the guys cleared out and told Ryan they would see him at school tomorrow.

Ryan was still smiling when his dad slammed him against the locker and said, "Why are you feeling so smug? You missed eight shots. What kinda college do you think is going to want you? And then, on top of that, you passed off six different times when you could've gone for a three pointer."

Ryan tried to explain that he wasn't sure he would get the shot, so he wanted his teammates to get a chance to score.

"Who are we concerned about getting a scholarship? You or your teammates? What else are you going to give away, Ryan? First, the Student Council election and now basketball games!" With that, his dad stormed out, leaving Ryan standing there stunned and alone.

After he finished sharing with Jennifer, Ryan waited for her to respond. There was another long pause when she realized she'd better say something.

"Ryan, any parent would have been thrilled with that kind of performance. It's obvious your dad wasn't feeling like himself or he's under some kind of pressure."

"Oh yeah. He's under some pressure all right. I caught him in the parking lot of his office a few weeks ago with his secretary as she was leaving to go home and they weren't exactly shaking hands good-bye."

"Did he see you?"

"Oh yeah. After she left, he threatened me with everything he could think of if I told my mom... Jennifer no one knows this, so you have to promise me you won't tell anyone."

"Of course, Ryan. You can trust me. I don't get my kicks hurting people."

"Touché, Jennifer. Gotcha. Why do you think men do those kinds of things?"

Jennifer proceeded to share what she thought. Ryan was totally into the conversation. Jennifer shared her idea of a healthy relationship where both people learn to give and think outside of themselves. They exchanged their ideas back and forth about what makes a relationship work until they realized they had been on the phone for over an hour, the math project unfinished.

"Jennifer, we haven't gotten anything done. Can I come over?"

"To my trailer? You, Ryan Rydell, who only recently egged it?"

"Yeah, okay, I was just trying to show off to my friends, and that was the same night I had caught my dad. I was trying to blow off some steam."

"So you took it out on me?"

"Guess so. I can't help Miss Wagner put me with you. We've got to get this project done. I want to play for Duke or Wake in college, and neither one will take me unless I get my math grades up. So, what's it gonna be?"

"Let me check with my parents...All right. They said if it was okay with me, then it was okay with them."

Leaving his wealthy neighborhood in Kings Crossing, riding his bike over to Jennifer's trailer in Tower Circle, Ryan thought about their conversation. Although he would never admit it to his friends because it would destroy his "macho" reputation, Ryan had enjoyed talking to Jennifer. He couldn't believe how much he had shared about his dad, but he knew Jennifer wouldn't rat him out. What surprised him more was how his heart jumped when he rode up to her trailer. She was standing out in the yard; the wind was blowing her hair all around, and for the first time, he really looked at her face. *You know, man, she's not bad except for those teeth.*

He put down his bike, walked over to Jennifer, locked eyes with her, and said, "Thanks for listening." Maybe it was the moonlight stirring up his heart, but the next thing he knew, he was taking Jennifer's face in his hands, giving her the first romantic kiss he had ever shared with a girl. They both were breathless for a moment.

Finally, Jennifer broke the spell that had come over them both; she led them back to the original reason Ryan was there. "Hey, we'd better get on that math before it's midnight."

"Yeah, let's."

On the way home, Ryan beat himself up. *I can't believe I kissed a loser. I'll make sure she knows I just lost my head tomorrow at school.*

Following through on his promise, Ryan pulled Seth into a huddle outside of Miss Wagner's door as the first period bell rang and Jennifer rounded the corner. She and Ryan locked eyes, glanced at each other, and for an instance there was a sparkle of hope in Jennifer's heart until Ryan quickly killed it. He looked back at Seth, and said, "Make way for Beaver Girl. We wouldn't want to be cut down by those teeth."

To his amazement, Jennifer didn't break down and cry; she just marched by, disgusted. He realized maybe she was tougher than what he'd thought. But he had an image to maintain, and she was not going to be part of ruining it. After they presented their project today, it would be the last time he would acknowledge her presence. He had big dreams for glory, and "Beaver Girl" and most popular guy don't work just like a math problem with the wrong variables. He dismissed her from his mind. At least he thought he did.

# JOY

As for the rest of the Student Body, students began to treat each other with kindness and weren't as tolerant when others were called names or mocked. Eye rolling lessened. Students even found themselves correcting their parents when they were gossiping maliciously about someone they knew or putting another person down.

Jake Williams shaved his head in support of his friend, Joy Johnson, who was fighting cancer. Joy had been diagnosed in the sixth grade. This year, she found herself battling for her life. Jake and Joy had been best friends since they were three years old. Once Jake shaved his head, his group of friends did as well, followed by other groups of guys. After a few weeks, there was a sea of young bald guys.

Jake had seen Abby in the hall and told her that Joy had asked about her. Abby said she was planning to go that night to visit her. She explained to Jake that after her dad's death, she had been very hesitant to set foot in a hospital. The night of her dad's death, she had to go to the hospital with her mom to identify her dad's body. Her mom had been hysterical.

Abby missed Joy, so she made up her mind she would go see her in the dreaded, heartbreaking hospital. She asked her mom if she could take Jennifer with her for support. Her mom said that was fine. She said having another person along would help her cope as well. Later that evening, the three of them set off for NorthEast Medical Center.

When they entered the room, Abby was shocked to see how much weight Joy had lost, but she did her best "Julia Roberts" imitation and didn't let Joy know she was startled.

"Hey, Joy. You're looking good," Abby said as she hugged her.

"Abby Legna, you're lying and you know it. Mrs. Legna, you can't let Abby lie like that. We all think she's perfect," Joy said, breaking the tension. They all laughed.

"Joy, this is Jennifer Alley. She's new to Concord Middle this year. She has something in common with you, because she loves to sing. Since you haven't been able to come to church, I thought you might enjoy hearing her sing something," Abby said.

"Yeah, that would be awesome. Nice to meet you, by the way, Jennifer."

"Nice to meet you, Joy," Jennifer said.

Abby wondered if Jennifer would get a different perspective on herself when faced with Joy's illness.

They were all looking face to face with someone who clearly didn't have long to live.

"Before you sing something, Jennifer, I have to tell you guys something. Jake told me you beat Ryan and you're the Student Body President. Congratulations, Abby," Joy said.

"Thanks, Joy. Sorry you couldn't be my campaign manager, but Jennifer did a good job filling in for you."

"Hey, that's cool. Well, you know how every year the president leads the class in a service project at Christmas?"

"Yeah, so?" Abby said.

"Well, I wondered if you would do something for me this year."

"What, Joy?" Joy's mom had walked in then, curious about what they were discussing.

"You know the organization Locks of Love?"

"Yes," they all said.

"They called me today. I had called them and left a message, asking them how many children were on the waiting list for wigs and how much it would cost. When they called back, they told me there are eight children waiting for wigs; the children don't have to pay. All their expenses are taken care of by donation," Joy said excitedly. "So, my request is that you guys take on Locks of Love for your service project and see how much money you can raise. I told them I was going to make sure those kids got their wigs so they could go to school and not be embarrassed."

"But you never wore a wig, Joy. Why is it so important to you?" Mrs. Legna asked.

"Mrs. Legna, I have known I was a miracle of God from the day I was born. Unfortunately, many kids don't get that; they think too much about how they look. I want to make it as easy for them as possible. Maybe if they got a prayer answered, it would open them up to hearing about God."

"Joy, that's so cool. I think we can do take your challenge on," Abby said, smiling.

"Great.

"Okay, then. I'm ready for my song, Jennifer," Joy said.

"What would'ya like me to sing?"

"Jesus Loves Me."

"Sure, Joy." Jennifer began to sing softly. As she sang, a huge smile came over Joy. She fell asleep, far removed from the group still standing around her bed. Her mom explained that she had taken a huge emergency dose of radiation in an effort to turn the cancer around. The doctor had doubted it would do any good. Joy had told them not to worry about her. She was going to do good whether or not the medicine did. Mrs. Johnson said she had no idea what she was talking about until now. Jake had been with her right after school. Mrs. Johnson said that must have been when Locks of Love called, because she hadn't been out of the room any other time during the day.

The reality of the situation hit Mrs. Johnson; she

began to cry. All the women in the room surrounded her with a huge group hug.

Back at school, Abby quickly went to work on the service project. One of the local professional football players for the Carolina Panthers, Kenny Delaney, read Joy's request in the *Charlotte Observer*. He organized a rally that received even more media coverage. An account was set up by Bank of America, where people could send in donations. When Kenny found out from Joy's parents that her school was trying to raise money, he went to his fellow football players and asked them if they would be willing to play in a celebrity golf tournament to try to meet Joy's goal. When the majority of them agreed, he called Abby and told her she needed to get runners to work the tournament, passing out drinks and snacks for the players. Abby then asked the Student Council. A vote was taken; the students agreed to work the tournament. Not only were they in support of the cause, but this was a great chance to rub shoulders with big name people. There was tremendous excitement and energy in the air. Those who agreed to participate were psyched about helping Joy encourage other sick children.

Kenny also contacted his best friend, Brent Larson. Brent was now a producer for *Oprah*. Brent and Kenny had played professional football together for the Chicago Bears before Brent busted his knee in a brutal sack. Kenny and Brent had been more than teammates; they had developed a deep friendship. Shortly after Brent was released from the team and went to work on *Oprah*, Chicago released Kenny too. The desperate Carolina Panthers took a chance on Kenny, signing him as a free agent, consequently, reviving his career. The fans in Charlotte had embraced him. He was anxious to give something back to the community.

Brent thought Kenny's idea was great. He wanted Kenny to fly up with Joy to Chicago to do a small segment on the show about people who were trying to make a difference in their communities. He booked them for the next week.

Joy's cancer spread; she continued to spiral downward. She deteriorated to the point where she was too weak to travel to Chicago. A crew came to film Joy from her room with Abby, Joy's parents, Kenny, Jake, and representatives from Locks of Love. When this clip aired, it also gave the Bank of America fund information. The exposure from *Oprah* combined with the success of Kenny's golf tournament caused the funds to come flooding in.

Joy's cheering squad rushed to the hospital to tell her. The latest report from the doctors had been bleak. They predicted Joy had at best two to three more days to live. Soon she would be incoherent due to the huge doses of pain medication.

Joy's mom informed Joy that she had a surprise in store for her in the afternoon. It had been hard to get Joy's attention due to a drug-induced catatonic state. Joy's mom appeared distraught.

"We have to get her awake for this announcement. It will give her so much peace," she said as Joy's friends entered the room. "What are we going to do?"

Jake responded that he had an idea. He asked Kenny and Abby if they could give him forty-five minutes. "Of course," they all said. Almost to the exact minute, Jake returned forty-five minutes later with Jennifer. Jake whispered his plan in Joy's mom's ear. Mrs. Johnson hugged Jake and told him to proceed. Jennifer started singing "Jesus Loves Me." Joy began stirring. She sat right up in bed, looked at them, and asked if they saw Him.

"Saw who?" they asked.

"Jesus. Do you see Him standing right there at the end of my bed? Mom, you do, don't you?" Joy asked.

Joy's mom had tears streaming from her eyes and was too choked up to answer. Joy looked bewildered, so Abby and Kenny decided to go forward with their announcement.

"Joy, we have something for you," Abby and Kenny said.

"What?" Joy asked.

"A check made out for twenty-five thousand dollars for Locks of Love. The eight kids they told you about will now receive wigs, and many more kids will in the future too," they said joyfully.

"That's awesome," Joy said. "Thank you so much. I'm ready to go too. Jesus is there at the end of the tunnel telling me it's time. I love you guys." When she finished speaking, Joy closed her eyes for the last time.

Seeing their friend and daughter die frightened them. Jake broke the silence, screaming out in the hospital room, "No, Joy, you can't leave me! You can't leave me!" over and over again until his voice was hoarse. Mr. and Mrs. Johnson tried to console him. After the screaming ended, he began to weep to the point of convulsing. Mrs. Legna had asked Abby to call Jake's parents to come for him. When they arrived, Jake was still out of control. His dad, Mike, with no other alternative, had to carry him out of the room.

As the weeks passed after Joy's death, Jake did not improve. He missed twenty school days, calling in sick; his grades were terrible. Mr. and Mrs. Johnson would call him at home to talk to him, but he always refused their calls. Finally, Mrs. Johnson had had enough; she drove over to the Williams' home to see him. When Jake's mom, Catherine, let her in, the two women embraced warmly, while Mike, his dad, went to Jake's room to get him. Jake said he didn't want to come out. Mrs. Johnson said that was fine with her, but she was coming in. She asked Jake's parents if she could have some time with Jake alone. They gave their permission, although they were nervous about how he might respond.

"Jake Williams," Mrs. Johnson began, "I have known you since you were three years old. You're like a son to me. I know Joy was your best friend. But, Jake, you know Joy would be mad at you if she saw you throwing your life away like this when hers has been taken. You are dishonoring her by not celebrating the life you have been given. Her other friends are, and that's what she would want you to do."

Mrs. Johnson continued, "You know, I never knew how significant our choice of a name would be for our dear girl, but, Jake, she has given lots of people she didn't even know joy. She loved you, and, Jake, she would be furious at you if you didn't see hope for your future.

"If you truly love Joy, Jake, you don't want to let her death make you bitter. You need to let it make you better. As our church always says, 'Love God, love people, and pass it on.' You know you have your family here, but we love you as well. We want you to continue to be involved in our family and not pretend you don't know us.

"Jake, Joy continues to live when we share our memories of good times we had with her and laugh. Sometimes we'll cry when we talk about her, but that's okay. It shows us how dear she was to us. Jake, I don't want to lose another child I love right now. You need to return to the land of the living."

Mrs. Johnson then walked over to Jake, who still had his back to her, and gave him a huge hug. She felt some resistance leave his body; he hugged her back. She left his room, closed the door, and went into the kitchen where his parents waited, eager to hear what had happened. She shared with them what she had said to Jake and his response. They joined hands, praying that Jake's heart would soften.

Days and weeks flew by until November twenty-fourth. Mr. and Mrs. Johnson, who had been so strong up until this point, felt themselves backslide. They both found it hard to function that day. After they returned home from work, they were sitting in the kitchen not saying anything more than "yes" or "no" to each other's questions, when they heard the doorbell ring.

"Are you expecting a delivery today, Richard?" Mrs. Johnson asked.

"No, Dianne, I'm not," he said. "I have no idea who that could be."

"Well, I better go see," Mrs. Johnson said. She opened the door to find Jake on her doorstep holding a birthday cake with thirteen candles on it.

"Today's your daughter's birthday, isn't it?" he asked.

"Yes, it certainly is," Mrs. Johnson said.

"Well, your 'son' is here to help you celebrate her life," Jake said smiling.

Later on that evening, Mrs. Johnson wrote in her journal that the prayer she had prayed with Jake's parents had been answered on November twenty-fourth, Joy's thirteenth birthday. She wrote further that instead of mourning, they had all celebrated Joy's positive impact on their lives.

# MISS WAGNER'S PLAN
## CONTINUES

Christmas came and went. The months seemed to fly by, and as they did, Jennifer's confidence continued to increase. A type of quasi-acceptance had occurred. People began to say hello to her in the hallways and not look the other way when she walked by. She even smiled at some of them. Her confidence came from knowing they had no idea what was going to be in store for them at the upcoming talent show. She laughed about the plan Miss Wagner had concocted. Boy, would they be surprised. Her mind, like a video camera, played that fateful day back in slow motion. It was just a few months ago, but Jennifer felt like she had lived several lifetimes since hearing the plan.

"Okay, Miss Wagner," Abby said, "What gives?"

"Well, Abby," Miss Wagner began. "I found out a little secret about Jennifer from Mr. Shive." Mr. Shive was the chorus teacher at Concord Middle, a very accomplished musician.

"What do you mean?" Jennifer said, not sure she wanted to hear the answer.

"Oh, that you have the voice of an angel," Miss Wagner said. "I knew that you sang, but Mr. Shive had me listen to a tape he had made of you singing a solo in his class. I had no idea how gifted you are, Jennifer."

"I don't know about being gifted, but I do know that I love to sing more than anything," Jennifer said.

"So Jennifer is going to sing at the talent show?" Abby said.

"Yes, but with some help." Miss Wagner said.

"Go on!" both girls almost shouted.

"Here's the deal," Miss Wagner began, as she whispered her plan to the girls. "But you girls can't tell a single soul in advance. It has to be a complete surprise to the Student Body."

"Unbelievable," Jennifer blurted out.

"Awesome..." Abby said.

To think how things had changed in such a dramatic way for Jennifer made her feel like she should fall down at Miss Wagner's feet, but she knew how inappropriate that would be, so she just said, "Miss Wagner, you're awesome."

"Jennifer, in the story about perseverance, what you don't realize is that you're the caterpillar who is fighting for all her might to come out of the cocoon. When the struggling ends, the caterpillar is able to escape the confines of her past and soar into the air as the beautiful butterfly. Abby and I are just helping you get out so you can fly! You go home and practice and pray. God will give you the strength to get out of your cocoon and emerge victorious. When that happens, all the problems you have had will almost seem worth it because of the new person you will be. I care about you; however, this is the time in your life that you need to start caring for yourself and realize that *you do matter!*"

Miss Wagner continued, "When you realize this, then you'll have come full circle. You'll be able to repeat what I have done to help you with someone else later. If in return that person helps someone, the cycle continues. Can you see the potential?"

"Yes, ma'am, I do," Jennifer said, her mind racing.

"Just think of the impact you, Abby, and I can make in the world. One little person can make a difference. You've got to believe that, Jennifer. And, as the saying goes, 'Reach for the brass ring that is out there for you.' Abby and I will be there cheering you on."

"Yes, Jennifer, we will be. You *can* do it," Abby said.

"But will I be able to sleep until I do it?" Jennifer asked.

They all laughed.

# THE TALENT SHOW

Word got around school that something was up with the talent show. No one was sure what, but the students had been told to expect TV crews from all the local stations and even some that weren't local. Seth's dad owned the local Hilton Inn. He told Seth that Meredith Vieira from *The Today Show* had shown up with her entourage, followed by a producer from *Oprah* who had come to the front desk asking for directions to Concord Middle.

Jennifer, who had been practicing non-stop and thinking about Miss Wagner's plan, worried she would be laughed off the stage. She tossed and turned all night long until her alarm went off. She couldn't believe the moment she had envisioned in her mind over and over again was finally here. Her stomach flipped as if the butterflies literally were trying to get out. She wondered how she would feel when it was all over.

Abby imagined the faces of the students when the surprise was revealed. Oh, how she couldn't wait to see Seth's and Ryan's surprise.

Two p.m. finally arrived. The students filed into the auditorium. There was a slight buzz because the gossips had done their work. All kinds of rumors had been circulating as to what might be up. Some even speculated that Miss Wagner was going to have Jennifer announce she was getting married so everyone would think Jennifer was somewhat cool. The students were restless because the end of the school year was coming. It was hot outside. The auditorium, with all the students' sweaty bodies squeezed tightly together, felt stifling. Everyone wanted to be anywhere but school.

Abby, being the Student Body President, introduced each act. Most were mediocre and boring. Some had even been forced by their parents to perform; it was obvious they were humiliated and furious at their parents. One girl paused three different times while playing her piano piece, getting more and more frustrated with each mistake. She stomped off when she was finished instead of bowing.

Another boy was trying to play his violin when his bow cracked and, to the delight of the students, he yelled out, "Oh s—-!" They had to wait several minutes while the strings teacher went to look for another bow.

Side conversations started between friends while they were waiting. After the violinist finished, Abby announced that the moment of the big surprise had arrived. The curtain pulled back to reveal Jason Simpson, last year's "American Idol," in the middle of the stage. The crowd went wild. He waited for everyone to settle down.

"Hi, everyone. A year ago, I had the privilege of being on a show that made me a household name," Jason began.

The students cheered and clapped.

"However, it wasn't always that way, and even one of the judges on the show said at the beginning that I was one of the ugliest men he had every seen. Well, I think most of you know what happened. They found out I could sing, and they gave me a makeover. Most people think of makeovers for only girls, but I want you to know lots of guys have them. They gave me contacts, changed the color of my hair, and gave me some cool clothes.

"And you know what? All of a sudden, I was accepted. You know, that kinda bothered me, because I had learned about love and kindness many years before when I had decided to work with children with disabilities who can't give you much in return. I found out what love and acceptance truly are. It's when you are kind to someone without expecting anything back. I want to sing a song that helped make me well known and echoes Abby's desire for kindness on campus. The name of the song is 'On the Wings of Love.'"

Jason began to sing, mesmerizing the audience. At the beginning of the second verse, Jennifer walked out. There was a small gasp. She began to sing with Jason; the chattering quieted down. Halfway through the second lyric, Jason stopped singing and whispered to Jennifer to keep singing. She continued; her palms sweated, her heartbeat raced, but she slowly began to get more confident until she was belting out the refrain. When she finished, the audience jumped to its feet and screamed madly, "Go, Jennifer, go!"

After it was all over and the students went back to class, Abby gave Jennifer a hug, along with Miss Wagner and Jason.

"Thank you so much, Miss Wagner, Abby, and Jason," Jennifer said, "You've given me an experience I promise I'll never forget!"

"It was our pleasure, Jennifer. We want to see you continue singing in the future. You have the talent. You just have to go for it," Miss Wagner challenged Jennifer.

"But what about my teeth?"—the hurt still evident in Jennifer's voice.

"Funny, you should say that," Jason said. "I was telling one of my friends, Judy, about coming to North Carolina to be here. She told her husband, Phil, about you. Well, Phil happens to be an orthodontist, and he is going to put braces on your teeth," Jason said.

"But you live in Nashville, right?" Jennifer asked, knowing her family wouldn't have the required money for the plane fare.

"Yes, but Judy and Phil live here in Concord," Jason said. "Your parents have given him their permission. You go Monday during school to get your teeth fitted for your braces."

Jason continued, "And, this summer you are going to sing back-up on one of the songs on my upcoming CD. You will get your part in the mail from my manager in the next few weeks. By doing this, you will be able to earn some extra money for summer."

"Wow! Unbelievable!"

"Jennifer, I'm so happy for you," Abby said. Jennifer knew Abby's response was sincere.

"Abby, if you hadn't been living out what you were saying in your campaign about kindness, none of this would've happened. You were kind to me when I didn't have a friendly face to turn to at Concord Middle. You, Miss Wagner, and Miss Early truly are my angels."

At that point, the whole group embraced: Abby, Jennifer, Miss Wagner, and Jason. As they were hugging, the media surrounded them, firing questions. Brent Larson, the *Oprah* producer, asked Jason to sign a waiver giving them permission to air what they had filmed. Before he walked off, he asked, "What's up with your school? It seems like everyone is so kind. I've never seen this before. This is my second time here in one year. What gives?"

They all laughed and shrugged their shoulders.

Meredith Vieira was waiting for Jennifer and Jason to answer her questions about how they had hooked up. No one had realized before this day that

Miss Wagner and Jason had been college friends at the University of North Carolina at Charlotte majoring in education together before a TV breakout hit, *American Idol*, had derailed Jason's teaching career.

As for Jennifer, in one hour, she had gone from a nobody to someone who was going to be splashed across the nation via the media. Or, as Miss Wagner would say, she had gone from being "nothing" to "it" at the end of one glorious May school day.

After the talent show, students started acting like they believed in themselves; with the power of prayer, anything was possible. Seeing Jennifer in braces was a constant reminder. And, as Abby had hoped and requested, they started treating each other like each person mattered, because they realized they might be sitting in class with the next president, or, even better, the next "American Idol."

# THE REST OF THE STORY

When the royalties from Jason's best selling CD started coming in the next year, he was able to pay Jennifer a generous percentage. She turned the money over to her family, who was able to move out of the trailer park into a small development. Mr. Shive began to give Jennifer vocal training after school. As the years passed, Jennifer received more and more attention due to her voice. The braces came off when she was a freshman in high school; she found herself being asked out for dates—usually from boys who attended other schools, not Concord High. Ryan Rydell and Seth Hudson retained their status as popular guys; only a fool would risk their abuse by asking Jennifer out for a date.

Jennifer didn't seem to mind though; her performing kept her busy when she wasn't studying. Graduation day came at last. Jennifer was on her way to Vanderbilt in Nashville on a music scholarship. Abby had won the Merit Scholarship to Chapel Hill, where she was planning to study law. The two vowed they would stay in touch. In her speech as valedictorian, Abby had quoted Eleanor Roosevelt, reminding the students, "No one can make you feel inferior without your permission." Jennifer came up to her at the end and told her what a great speech it had been and how her mother used to quote Mrs. Roosevelt to her all the time in middle school.

Abby asked her, "Do you remember when I told you in the bathroom about how Ryan and Seth would reap what they'd sown one day?"

"Yeah, I remember," Jennifer said.

"Well, neither one of them got accepted into the college they wanted. They will both have to stay here and go to UNCC and try to transfer next year. Meanwhile, we're off to conquer the world, right, Jen?" Abby challenged Jennifer.

"Amen, sister." Jennifer had learned at Abby's church that "Amen" actually meant something. It meant, "And, so be it."

And, so it was.

However, before they embarked on their respective journeys, a graduation night to remember would turn into one they wished they could forget. Jennifer and Abby had been invited to a party at the Johnsons' home. Jake had decided after Joy's thirteenth birthday that his second family was going to participate in all the big events of his class. All of Joy's friends had decided they would spend their evening with their parents at the Johnsons' home.

Dinner was catered with lots of toasting and well wishing. Joy's parents had decided the toasting would be non-alcoholic because they didn't want their guests to be driving home afterwards with alcohol in their systems. Their wish for Joy's friends was that they could see it was possible to have fun without alcohol. The Johnsons realized the enormous pressures the kids had already been subjected to about drinking. The prevailing thought was still, if you were cool, you'd drink. Having lost their precious daughter, they couldn't understand how anyone would want to gamble with fate.

A few blocks over, another party was celebrating graduation. This party thought that graduation, being a rite of passage, demanded the presence of alcohol. Seth's and Ryan's dads had made sure there was plenty of booze for their boys, who were now passing into adulthood. Most of the parents were drunk themselves after an hour or so. When the food and the booze were gone, Ryan and Seth announced to their parents they were going to take their dates, Megan and Brooke, out dancing in Charlotte. They would be in by three a.m., they announced. Their parents waved them on, happy to see them enjoying themselves.

Later that morning, the Highway Patrol received a call about an SUV that had crashed into a tree on Sharon Road. The message was that the driver had apparently lost control of the car and one passenger had been thrown from the vehicle. When Patrol Sergeant Leach arrived at the scene, he told reporters open beer cans were all over the car. Once the ambulance was on its way, the parents had to be notified. Upon hearing the news, the Rydells, the Carters, the Stewarts, and the Hudsons made their way to the hospital, where they all paced up and down the floors of the emergency room, frantically waiting for news.

Finally, at six a.m., the world, which had seemed so joyous eight hours earlier, now seemed pretty bleak. Megan's parents were told she had died upon impact. Brooke's parents were told she had sustained injuries that would leave her paralyzed. The Hudsons were told when the car had run into the tree, Seth had suffered severe head trauma and would recover physically, but never mentally.

Ryan, who had been the driver, had suffered a concussion and would be kept overnight for observation. In the meantime, the doctors told his parents that the officers would need to question him as soon as he was conscious. After questioning, they would determine what charges Ryan would face.

Upon hearing the news, Mrs. Carter passed out. When she came to, she kept repeating over and over, "They're just kids. This can't be happening. They're just kids."

Sergeant Leach, who was standing over to the side with his partner, Dave, remarked, "You wouldn't put your little baby in the middle of a highway and tell him to go have a good time. Why would you put your child in a car knowing he or she had been drinking?" Dave shook his head. Then he remembered something he had seen in the paper a few days prior.

"Didn't Concord High have a student speak last week about how he had killed his buddy when they were out carousing because he had been drunk?"

"Yeah, this kid, Karl, tried to warn the students about the dangers of drinking and driving. He knew how strong the pull would be to party on graduation night, drink excessively, and then hop into a car and drive home impaired."

"Lotta good it did," Dave said.

"Well, you never know. Maybe it stopped some of the rest of the class from being here tonight in this situation. We know one group didn't listen. Maybe the majority did. There's always this idea with kids that bad stuff is not going to happen to them—that it happens to other people. You know, I'm invincible and you're not."

"Yeah, I thought that too," Dave said. "I just don't know how these families are going to deal with this."

"Me neither," Sgt. Leach said. "This would be a good time for a miracle."

"You believe in that crap, Leach?" Dave said.

"You bet, and if you know what's good for you, you'll try it out for yourself and stop mocking me," Leach challenged.

"Save the preaching for church and let's go see if we can do something for these traumatized families," Dave said.

"Yes, good idea. And, when we do, we will be ministering God's love," Sergeant Leach said.

"You're full of it," Dave shot back, but he did agree in his heart that a miracle was going to be needed here.

# THE MIRACLE

Megan's service was held the next Wednesday. The church was packed. Pastor Jim of First Assembly conducted the service. Jennifer sang "Jesus Loves Me." Those in attendance were completely unaware of the multitudes of angels who joined their midst as she sang, providing a hedge of protection around the seated guests. These "special guests" looked at each other as Jennifer was singing, and said, "Yes, He does." To which, He replied, "Yes, dear friends, I do love you, and them as well, *forever*. If this world could ever grasp how much, what a different place it would be."

After the service, Abby, Lauren, Jaqueline, and Jake came up and told Jennifer what a good job she had done. They were impressed she could do that for someone who had been so mean to her.

Jennifer said, "It was God that gave me the strength to do it. Otherwise, no way could I have done it. I do have feelings, you know."

It was obvious to Jennifer that Andrea and Ashlyn wanted to be a part of the group as they were standing over to their right listening, but not joining in. Jennifer decided to break the ice by saying, "Andrea and Ashlyn, I think we've all seen how valuable life is. Let's let bygones be bygones and start over. Whadd'ya say?"

They both sighed a sigh of relief and said, "Yes, let's."

"I've got an idea, guys," Abby said. "Let's go to the hospital and visit Seth."

They all agreed. When they got to the hospital, his mom was sitting with him. She told them he had not come out of the coma to respond to anything. Abby asked if she could pray for him. Mrs. Hudson said that was fine. Abby laid hands on him and asked God to heal Seth. She could feel his body heat as she prayed for him, but no physical response.

Over the summer, Abby and Jennifer continued to visit Seth. One day when they were in the room alone with him, Abby asked Jennifer to sing "Jesus Loves Me." As Jennifer began to sing, they both noticed Seth's eyes began to flutter. They ran down to the cafeteria to get Mrs. Hudson. When they returned to the room, Seth was unresponsive again. Shortly thereafter, he was moved to another facility for long-term patients.

One day his mom fell asleep while sitting beside his bed. When she woke up, she heard someone saying, "Man, you're pretty." She thought she was dreaming; she rubbed her eyes only to find Seth staring straight at her and smiling.

As the summer came to an end, Seth was out of bed learning to talk and walk again. As soon as he was aware of his surroundings, he asked what had happened to him. His parents went through the whole story. When they explained that Ryan had been driving, Seth sighed deeply.

"I kept having this dream I was the one who was driving. Now, I know why Ryan hasn't been to see me. Call his parents to tell him to come," Seth commanded. He also wanted to see Brooke. His parents explained she was in a different hospital; he would have to wait until he was given a pass from his doctors to leave the hospital temporarily.

Brooke, on the other hand, was fine mentally, but when she found out she was paralyzed, she shut down emotionally. She glared at anyone who came into her room. When she had visitors, she screamed at her mother to get them to leave. Brooke's mom waved them on, helpless and embarrassed, mouthing she was sorry. As college began for her classmates, Brooke wallowed in self-pity, still forbidding anyone to visit and wish her well.

Ryan refused to see anyone because he was drowning in guilt. Seth got up his nerve, called Ryan, and told him he knew he couldn't drive because his license had been taken, but he was going to come kick his butt if he didn't get his dad to drive him over. Ryan agreed to come. When Ryan and his dad got to the rehab hospital, Seth told them they were going to take a little drive. He had gotten permission to go on a three-hour pass, and they were taking him over to see Brooke.

When they got to Brooke's room, a smile flickered over her mouth. She had always adored Seth but had always played it low key prior to the accident. She had reacted before she had transformed herself into the angry persona. As soon as she realized she was smiling, she stifled it.

"Come on in," Mrs. Carter said, hoping Brooke wouldn't start screaming.

"Mom, tell them to leave," Brooke screamed.

Ryan was happy to and started out. Seth and his dad grabbed him.

"No, Missy, we're not leaving. It took me two months to get a pass, and you are the first person I've seen outside of the hospital. And, Miss Carter, you're looking marvelous, I might add."

Once again, it took all of Brooke's self-control to squelch her desire to laugh. "Missy," he had always playfully called her, "I know you remember Jennifer and how we went after her. Well, after our accident, I was in a coma. I heard her singing to me. I tried to respond, but all I could do was flicker my eyelashes. I was trying to say, 'I'm in here and I am coming out,' but I couldn't yet. Abby had laid hands on me, too, praying that God would heal me."

Seth then walked over to Brooke, placed his hands on her shoulders, and said, "I know you are in there, Missy, and I want you to come out."

This time, Brooke couldn't squelch it. A huge smile broke out as a tear rolled down her cheek.

At Thanksgiving, when Abby and Jennifer came home on break, much to their surprise, they found Seth giving Brooke wheelies in her wheelchair outside her hospital. Ryan had come by while they were there. He told Abby he was going to take her up on her invitation to come to church and would be there that Sunday. Keeping his promise, he did come and sit with Abby, but nothing extraordinary happened.

Abby and Jennifer linked up at home at the end of May before they started summer school. They went by to see Brooke and found out she was getting ready to be discharged. Her parents had made accommodations in their house. She would be able to get around in her motorized wheelchair. And, the best news, she said, was that The Office of Disability Services had secured a scholarship and aide for her. She would be starting school in the fall.

Seth walked in and said, "No, that's not the best news. The best news is that we are going to UNCC together," and he gave Brooke a big hug and kiss.

No one was surprised when three years later, once again, they were watching Seth give Brooke a big hug and kiss. But this one was before all their friends and family as Brooke Carter became Mrs. Seth Hudson, or "Missy" Hudson, as she came to be called more and more.

Many years later when a classmate asked Lauren where Brooke was at their thirtieth high school reunion, she corrected him, saying, "You mean Missy? She's on the dance floor with Seth, where else?"

At the same thirtieth high school reunion, Ryan danced with his gorgeous wife. Ryan thought how hard it had been to convince Jennifer to sing at their reunion. This time, she was the attractive one. He, on the other hand, had gained weight and lost his hair. No one would be eyeing him. Although Jennifer had had her teeth corrected, she still hesitated to be in the spotlight when it came to Concord, North Carolina. Getting her to agree to sing in front of her old classmates had been one of the hardest things Ryan had ever done. He had to admit she would have would've said no if Abby hadn't intervened. Asserting herself was no problem for Jennifer at this stage of her life.

When Ryan thought back on the hardest, gut-wrenching work he had ever done, which changed him from "party boy" to responsible citizen, he brought to mind a night many years prior when he stopped by to see Jim Benson at First Assembly.

Abby had introduced Ryan to Jim shortly after the car accident when he had visited her church. Abby explained to Ryan that their church had more than one pastor and Jim was the pastor for their age group—college and young adults. There was something about Jim that Ryan felt clicked with him. He seemed to be the first "non-fake" pastor he had ever met.

After Abby and Jennifer had taken off to college and Seth was caught up with his rehabilitation, Ryan spent much of time agonizing over the accident and its results. It seemed his dad had aged twenty years since the accident. All joy zapped out of him. It had humiliated Mr. Rydell to see his son, whom he had thought would achieve great things, tragically kill one friend and ruin the lives of two others. Mr. Rydell couldn't let go of the embarrassment. He retreated farther and farther into himself, alcohol being his only comfort. He hardly spoke to Ryan or anyone else anymore. Ryan's mom contemplated divorcing him.

Ryan felt so lonely, he thought about suicide. Every time he looked at his left hand, he had a visual reminder of the wreck. His hand had gone through the windshield as he hurtled forward upon impact with the tree. As a result, Ryan badly wounded his left hand and lip. His mom had suggested plastic surgery, but a part of him felt he should keep the scars so he would never forget what he had done.

In one of his lowest moments, Ryan remembered Pastor Jim, and he went to see him. His license had been reinstated, so he was able to drive himself. When he got to Jim's office, he remembered how Abby had bragged about Jim's ability to remember names after one meeting. He thought that was a bunch of bull until that moment when Jim looked up at him and said, "Hey, Ryan, what brings you to First Assembly on a Monday afternoon?"

"I really need someone to talk to, Pastor Jim, if you have a minute," Ryan said.

"Sure, I do, Ryan. I thought, after meeting you with Abby, you and I might get the opportunity to get to know each other better. What brings you here today?"

At that point, all the pain and guilt came flooding out from where Ryan had repressed it all these months. He began to weep with heart-piercing sobs.

Pastor Jim sensed he needed to do this; he didn't say anything. He waited for Ryan to compose himself in order to continue the conversation.

"Pastor Jim," Ryan began. "My dad loses no opportunity to remind me that I killed one person and ruined the lives of two others. And, on top of that, he says, I ruined my chance for making something out of myself; he says that I am doomed to be a loser."

"Do you believe you're a loser, Ryan?" Pastor Jim asked curiously.

"Honestly, I don't know what I believe anymore. I know that I am filled with guilt about Megan, Seth, and Brooke."

"Ryan, have you asked Seth, Brooke, and Megan's parents to forgive you?"

"No, sir, I haven't. I know they hate me."

"You might be surprised, Ryan. No one made them drink that night. They had a free will to do whatever they wanted to that night. You didn't hold them at gunpoint and force them to ride with you. They went because they wanted to. You just happened to be the one driving. Megan could have been the one driving, and you could be the one dead. You all made bad choices that night, Ryan. All of you. *All of you*," Pastor Jim repeated for emphasis.

"I see your point," Ryan said, his head between his knees, held in a tight grip by his hands. "What do I do now?"

"You leave here, go to each of them, and tell them you are sorry about what happened. You ask each of them to forgive you. Then, you meet back with me tomorrow afternoon, and we will discuss what has happened," Pastor Jim said.

Ryan felt a sense of direction for the first time in months. He knew Pastor Jim was right. He had to make amends with those involved. How they would respond would be up to them, he understood from Pastor Jim, but before God, he had to ask for their forgiveness.

Ryan feared the Stewarts' reaction the most, so he headed for Brooke and Seth's house first. When he got there, Seth gave him a big hug and directed him to the living room. Brooke was already in there painting. She had always been a good artist. While at UNCC, an aide had told her about art classes for the disabled. She enrolled and learned how to hold the brush in her teeth. Her family members were amazed at what she was able to do.

Seth showed Ryan a painting. It was of three

little girls. Brooke explained that God had given her the faces of these three girls in a dream. She did not know them yet, she explained, but she felt she would in the future. Seth had a sad look cross his face, but just as quickly, his smile returned. Ryan knew he was thinking that they would never have their own children. The guilt began to suffocate him all over again. He was tempted to run out. Seth then propelled him to the reason he was there.

"What brings you to the Hudson home today, my man? You know you're welcome here anytime, but you look like you have a mission. You're all serious looking," Seth said, trying to get Ryan to lighten up.

"Well, Seth and Missy, it's a serious thing that brings me here. I haven't been able to do it until today, because I've been drowning in guilt about the accident. I got to where I couldn't take it anymore, and I've come to ask if there's any way you guys could forgive me?"

Seth responded first, "Ryan, my man, if you'd been sweating over me all this time, you should've talked to me about it. I got rid of all my anger in that coma. I tell you that when Abby laid hands on me, I came out a different, but better person. I forgave you a long time ago, dude."

There was a long pause before Brooke finally spoke.

"Ryan, I have to be honest and tell you that I'm not thrilled to be paralyzed. I hate it, but I don't blame you. We'd all been drinking. You just happened to be the one at the wheel. Maybe if one of us had been driving, we all would've been killed. I have definitely come to see how valuable life is, and this terrible accident brought Seth to confess his love to me. Who knows? We may have gone our separate ways to college and forgotten about each other, but I love him so much, Ryan; like him, there is a new person here. I am Missy now, and I'm okay with that. Seth and my painting give me great joy."

Missy continued, "I wish I could walk, but I deal with it. I, too, forgave you long ago. For me, it was when you visited that time with Seth and your dad. Seth got me to laugh for the first time in months. You, on the other hand, looked like you were at death's doorstep. I remember feeling sorry for you and your dad. Go on and live your life, Ryan, and make something good come out of this tragedy." Missy rolled over to Ryan and gave him a big kiss on the cheek.

"Thanks guys," Ryan said as tears streamed down his face. "There are two other people I need to see tonight."

Seth led him to the door and said, "It's going to be okay, Ryan; have faith."

"Yeah, man, I believe it is," Ryan said as he hugged Seth tightly in a warm embrace. "I'm so sorry man." He let go of Seth and sprinted to his car to avoid breaking down again.

Finding Ryan at their doorstep surprised the

Stewarts even more. As they listened to his request, they assured him they, too, had forgiven him a long time ago. They shared with Ryan they had learned that holding onto their anger was not going to bring Megan back. They had to let her and the anger go, too, or they were not going to be able to live either.

They also challenged Ryan to make something out of his life and not let Megan's death be in vain. They had been comforted by the news Abby delivered to them shortly after Megan's funeral. Joyfully, they told Ryan that Megan had gone on a youth retreat to the beach with First Assembly two weeks before graduation. There she had made a profession of faith to Pastor Jim, who spoke at her funeral and assured everyone she was in the presence of Jesus, suffering no more.

They told Ryan their latest discovery and what Jim preached gave them some degree of peace. They shared that several days after her funeral, when they had gotten their courage up to go in her room, they had found Megan's Bible open to the 23rd Psalm and a journal describing her new faith. She said in the journal entry that she had always sung "Jesus Loves Me" robotically, but on the retreat, Jennifer and Abby had challenged her to say the words to herself aloud and ponder their meaning. In them, they told her, the whole Gospel could be summarized. *I came to understand that day*, she wrote, *that He truly does love me; I am indeed thankful.*

When Ryan left, his heart was full. He had

thought he would never taste happiness again. *Wow, Pastor Jim had been so right.* He couldn't wait until the next day to tell him.

As Ryan bounced into Pastor Jim's office and relayed to him the next day what had happened, Pastor Jim began to smile.

"What are you smiling about?" Ryan asked.

"Just that our God is an awesome God, Ryan. He's fulfilling Romans 8:28 right before you."

"What does that say, Pastor Jim? I'm not Bible literate quite yet."

Pastor Jim laughed and said, "A person can study the Bible his whole life and not be Bible literate. There is so much there, Ryan. Plus, you need the Holy Spirit to interpret the Word for you. Here is what the verse I referenced says: 'And we know that in all things God works for the good of those who love him, who have been called according to his purpose.'"

Pastor Jim continued, "Have you ever thought, Ryan, that there was a reason you were spared? That God might have a purpose for your life; that by using you, the lives of Megan, Brooke, and Seth might be honored? Have you ever thought that maybe you could convert the dead to life?"

Now, Ryan knew enough to know this sounded blasphemous, but Pastor Jim went on to explain what he meant. As he listened to Pastor Jim, a joy he had never known leapt into Ryan's heart. He now knew what he was supposed to do. He had a strong sense for the first time what the plan and purpose for his life was. It was ever so clear.

# EPILOGUE

We are privileged today to have Jennifer Alley on our show. Jennifer, last night, won a Grammy for her latest CD entitled, 'Celebrating Life,'" Sasha Osafor announced at the beginning of *The Today Show*.

"Jennifer, tell our viewers what it was like for you winning your first Grammy," Sasha said.

"Well, it was pretty exciting," Jennifer said.

"Was it life changing?"

"To tell you the truth, Sasha, there was a competition I won twenty-five years ago that was truly life changing, but it wasn't the Grammys," Jennifer said.

"What do you mean?"

"Well, this competition goes way back to my days as a seventh grader at Concord Middle School," Jennifer said.

"Tell us more, please," Sasha begged. "Didn't you and the president become friends during middle school?"

"Yeah, that's right. Having Abby as a friend really changed my life," Jennifer said.

"Go on..." Sasha pleaded.

"You know, Sasha. There are a lot of people out there that have talent. But our society puts so much stock in appearance, it makes it difficult for some of them to 'make it.' I was in that category, and if it weren't for Abby, I wouldn't be sitting here."

"What do you mean exactly, Jennifer?"

"Abby was blessed as a kid. She was beautiful and still is; she was smart, and still is, which is evident now in difficult decisions she makes. She could've been really cocky, but she wasn't. Her parents had instilled in her values of a different realm. They taught her that the things of this world aren't significant. They taught her that all she would leave behind would be a legacy of how she treated people and impacted her world for good. They frequently said, at her funeral, no one would talk about how big her house was, or what kind of car she drove. People at the end of her life would talk, instead, about the kind of person she was."

Jennifer continued, "Abby really strove to live those values out, especially after her dad died. When I met her, I was an ugly seventh grader with really buckteeth. I always joked with her that she was my guardian angel sent by God; the proof was in her last name—Legna—which is 'angel' spelled backwards."

"Legna being Abby's maiden name is a pretty cool coincidence. So, Jennifer, you're kinda like the story of 'The Ugly Duckling?'" Sasha inquired. "Or, as *People Magazine* dubbed you, 'From Beaver to Beauty.'"

"Exactly," Jennifer laughed. She continued, "With the help of my teacher, guidance counselor, and Abby, I was able to develop enough confidence to try out for my school's spring talent show. Winning that contest was truly the highlight of my life, because no one at that school, except those three and a couple others, knew I could sing. They couldn't look beyond the buckteeth. When I sang in front of them for the first time, they were utterly amazed and gave me a standing ovation—my first and most memorable one. The rest is history, as the cliché goes," Jennifer chuckled.

"With all the rage about plastic surgery these days and looking our youngest, that's truly refreshing," Sasha said.

"Yes, wouldn't it be cool if people judged each other according to one's heart instead of appearance?" Jennifer asked.

"Indeed, that would be the ideal world," Sasha said. Changing the subject, Sasha asked, "I did read that you give away ninety percent of your income. Why do you do that?"

"When my mom died, I was helped through my grief by the music of a Christian singer, Rich Mullins. Rich gave almost all of his money away until he was tragically killed in a car accident. After his death, a Legacy Fund was established to continue his work with young people. I told myself that if I ever made it, I would emulate him because he was truly my hero. Then, a classmate of ours was also killed in a car accident when we were in high school. She had just committed her life to the Lord. Of course, her parents were devastated. Abby and I told her parents we would find a way to honor her memory. That's why we decided to name our fund The Megan Stewart Scholarship Fund.

"Well, I know there are some really grateful kids out there," Sasha said. "Didn't I read in the *People* article that Megan was one of the girls who bullied you, yet you named one of your daughters after her? Why?"

Jennifer nodded and laughed. "My Megan, who is eight, asked me the same thing after she read the *People* article. I explained to her the redemptive power of our Lord. I told her that although Megan had been a bully before her death, she had been transformed and now was in glory with Him. She was, indeed, a new creation."

"What do you personally get out of putting your money in this scholarship fund?"

"If these kids will help someone down the road, then this pattern of giving becomes a perpetual cycle. The potential is there to radically impact our world for good, if we are willing to move out of the restrictions society tries to impart," Jennifer said.

"My parents dreamed of seeing me graduate from college—something they'd never had an opportunity to do. Each kid who graduates helps me know that my mom and dad had a plan and a purpose for their lives that was bigger than either of them realized when they were here on this earth. But, you know what, Sasha?" Jennifer continued, "They're wearing the biggest crowns you have ever seen right now; they're looking down at these kids and grinning great big smiles that only people from the hills of West Virginia know how to do. When I think about their influence, I get one of those great big smiles on my face as well, and I think to myself, *ain't life good?*"

"Yes, it is. And, Jennifer, I found a high school friend from your past who said that our viewers would find it interesting to know who your business manager is," Sasha probed.

"Seth Hudson," Jennifer said.

"Why is he significant?" Sasha said.

"Because he and his buddy, Ryan Rydell, did everything in their power to put me down in middle school, along with Megan and her group. Now, Seth manages my finances, along with his wife, Brooke. They also help with my girls, Joy, Faith, and Megan, when I am on the road touring, and my husband comes along.

"And who's your husband and what does he do?" Sasha said.

"Well, you could say that my husband converts the dead to life," Jennifer said.

Confused, Sasha asked, "What do you mean?"

"He's a pastor. Actually, he's not just the pastor of any church. He's the pastor of the biggest church in Nashville. Miracles are always happening there."

"But you didn't say his name? Are you ashamed of him?"

"Absolutely not. My husband is the best-looking guy you've ever seen. Though Abby and I disagree about whose husband is the best looking."

"His name?"

"Ryan Rydell."

Sasha couldn't recover quickly enough from the shock to reply or ask another question, so her producer went to a commercial to give her time to regroup.

Lying in her bed with the covers pulled tightly to her face while vacationing in southern Florida, the TV blaring, exhorting the viewer to have cleaner clothes with Tide, a proud Miss Wagner said, "That's my girl, Jennifer. You did it. You kept the circle going."

"Whoa, Brett, I never knew Abby and Jennifer were BFFs for so long!"

"Excuse me? I'm not up on that term."

"It's an acronym for 'Best Friends Forever.'"

"Oh, yeah, they have been since middle school,

but they would also tell you that Jesus Christ is their all time BFF. You know, Cassie, Abby and I are coming to the end of our gig here. What I hope you take away from their story is this: it's no coincidence you're our assistant. It's a God thing. Like the BFFs of our story, make your legacy count for eternity. This is your time, Cassie. You can make the world a better place because you were here."

"Wow, Brett, I don't know if I can, but I will definitely try."

# ENDNOTES

1. "10 Things God Doesn't Care About."
Anonymous prose circulated via the Internet.

# AUTHOR BIO

Jennifer Calvert has worked in the field of education for over twenty years. She has worked with elementary, middle, and high school students. She currently is the Lower School Counselor at Cannon School in Concord, North Carolina. She holds a B.A. in Spanish from Wake Forest University and a Master's Degree of Education in the field of counseling from Western Carolina University. She and her husband, Dave, reside in Concord with their daughter, Cassie. In her free time, Jennifer loves to exercise and enjoy life with her family and friends.